THE GATES OF VALHALLA

JASPER GRAWL

THE GATES OF VALHALLA

JASPER GRAWL

ILLUSTRATED BY YUKI ISHII

Fresh Ink Group

Roanoke

The Gates of Valhalla

Fresh Ink Group
An Imprint of:
The Fresh Ink Group, LLC
PO Box 525
Roanoke, TX 76262
Email: info@FreshInkGroup.com
www.FreshInkGroup.com

Edition 1.1   2014

Book design by Ann Stewart

Front Cover Design and Illustrations by Yuki Ishii

Back Cover design by Reymond Mendez

Author Photo by Shingo Maehara

Cataloging-in-Publication Recommendations: FICTION/General;
FICTION/Satire; FICTION/Humor;
FICTION/Science Fiction/General;
FICTION/Science Fiction/Alternative History;
FICTION/Political; FICTION/Dystopian;
FICTION/Literary; FICTION/Literary Farce

Library of Congress Control Number: 2013957744

ISBN-13:978-1-936442-18-8

To my Mom,

cuz she's the best.

ACKNOWLEDGMENTS

My most sincere, abiding, and effusive thanks:

To Mother and Father, who got the ball rolling, so to speak.

To my book designer, Ann Stewart, my editor, Stephen Geez, and the entire team at Fresh Ink Group, who did all the nuts-and-bolts work to get this sucker out.

To Yuki Ishii, who is creative and talented and smart.

To Natalie, Pete, and T (word), who were patient enough to read this thing raw, and kind enough to tell me what they didn't like about it.

To Mrs. T, who bludgeoned me with grammar for three unrelentingly merciless years; Ms. S, who made me believe that I was actually a good writer, and Mr. W, who made sure that I knew I wasn't; and to Mr. F, who was passionate about music and sports and history and making people laugh. He showed me how it was done.

To Mom and Dad, Ben, and Chelsea, who clothed and fed and cared for me; who taught me how to bait a hook and how to keep my head down and how to deep fry an entire turkey in one go; who survived The Calamitous Yellowstone Expedition of '91 in the car with me; who cleaned up my messes and never spilled the beans; who made the French toast soggy, just like I like it; who blind-squirrel-finds-a-nutted themselves into championship-game victories; who plays a mean game of Scrabble; and who are my biggest fans.

To you, generous reader, who are giving me the time of day.

To Clay, who *still* owes me $125 for fantasy football.

And to everyone else. I couldn't have done it without you.

IN THE BEGINNING . . .

Clocks are much like angry gorillas. Find yourself seques-
tered away in a room with either one and chances are it will
be the first thing you notice. Furthermore, the larger it—the
clock *or* the gorilla—is, the greater the importance placed on
said noticing. The similarities end at size and salience,
though. Clocks are universally accepted to be far more
dangerous and exceedingly more malevolent than any
maddened ape. Ask anyone. All one needs to do to survive
an altercation with a cross gorilla is make an offering of
peace; bananas are best. Clocks, on the other hand, rank
among the cruelest, most sinister contrivances ever con-
cocted.

As a general rule, clocks are detested and feared. And
for good reason. Most consider them to be a form of

excruciatingly cruel punishment. On Earth, in fact, the first clock was created by an enterprising young human named Ghhyh for the purpose of being used as the first weapon of mass destruction. Ghhyh and his fellow men and women had really hit the jackpot. They were the sole inhabitants of a tropical island paradise. Mind you, this was way back before Man had developed any form of spoken language. There weren't even loin-cloths or coconut brassieres. Men and women just pranced around innocently, their floppier bits fluttering listlessly in warm tropical zephyrs. All Ghhyh and his buddies did, all day, every day, was lie on pristine white-sand beaches, eat bananas, and fornicate. The men liked fornicating. The women liked fornicating. And everyone loved the bananas. It was a real sweet setup—like the Garden of Eden. Heck, it *was* Eden.

Most people would be content to live out the rest of their days in this dreamland banana orgy, but not ole Ghhyh. One day, while he was sitting atop the highest hill on the island, a half-eaten plantain in one hand and a libidinous, nubile lovetress in the other, Ghhyh happened upon another tropical island paradise just across the water. Blessed with the eyes of a carrot-eating hawk and taking full advantage of his lofty perch, Ghhyh could clearly see, for the first time, his neighbors. On the opposite beach was a tribe of buxom women—naked, fornicating, and eating bananas. Instantly, greed crept into Ghhyh's heart. He wanted those bananas.

An insidious thought sidled up to Ghhyh's prefrontal cortex: *If he were going to get a hold of those bananas he would need a weapon.* From this moment forward the poor, wretched inhabitants of the planet Earth would no longer be afforded the luxury to dilly and dally though life. Never again would they bask in the rays of perpetual laziness unburdened by fear or reproach. From that moment on, they would be late.

After a fortnight of tinkering away in his beach-side work bungalow, Ghhyh presented his weapon to the village elders. He had constructed the first working sundial out of a banana peel and a banana leaf with some banana smudges on it. He attempted to explain that the smudges were numbers by which one could measure the amount of time that had passed by looking at the shadow cast upon the leaf, but since there was no language in which he could iterate his point, no one could decide if he was really on to something big or if he had just had the wind knocked out of him. It wasn't until he picked up a banana and opened his hands wide as if he were a mime moving a sofa—the universal sign for "many"—then pointed to the beach across the water, that everyone got all gung-ho for invasion.

The doomsday device was pre-emptively drifted over in the dead of night on a mass of floating peels. Eighty-three fateful hours later, the malignancy of Time metastasized. By then, many more clocks had already been replicated and reproduced so no one, anywhere, could escape the suffocating sleeper hold of the Great Thief. These clocks siphoned off the seconds and minutes of the day like unregulated money managers, perniciously directing each man, woman, child, and banana closer to the end, one smudgety-tock at a time. They burgled away every passing moment, sucked off every instant, and broadcast maliciously the ever-decreasing interval between the blissful dregs of vacations and first days back to work. Alarms daily roused every weary soul from their slumber to remind all just how much time they didn't have to sleep. Language sprouted up overnight simply to express by what degree everyone was late for this or tardy for that. Ever vigilant, Time marched on.

Eventually the clocks determined that it was time to strike Ghhyh and all his buddies before they got any ideas about stealing the bananas—or worse, putting people behind. Not having the slightest clue of how to understand what time to expect the attack, Ghhyh watched helplessly as his island was overrun. The men were killed and all the bananas were commandeered. The women were raped. There was no time for love-making. Everything was going according to Schedule.

I

The Big Prologue

5 . . . 4 . . . 3 . . . 2 . . . 1 . . . "pip"

• • •

"O RDER! ORDER, please! Would you all take your seats!" shouted the Speaker. He was a prim man, long in the face, whose cheeks swung low off his jaw like gravity-laden chariots. Behind him and above his head was mounted a digital clock, having just passed five minutes on its way to zero. The timepiece was at least twice the size of a Texas fish story, and the first thing everyone noticed upon entering the chamber.

"Let's get this thing over with. I'm sure that we all have more pressing matters to attend to. Don't make me use the gavel!" threatened the Speaker, waiving his mallet in a cloud of menacing ill-humor. His golf bag propped up yearningly behind the podium, he attempted to usher the other members to their seats. If the indignant scowl on his sagging face did not shout *It's going to take a miracle for me to make my 8:42 tee time,* his plaid knickers and hideous moleskin sweater certainly did. As a licensed golfer the Speaker was required to abide the strictest adherence to the most sprawling, all-encompassing set of archaic bureaucratic regulations outside of those required to order a gyro from an agitated Greek vendor at bar time. Ironically, this didn't prohibit him from dressing like furniture from the 1960s.

"Gentlemen! Gentlemen! Do we have to do this every time?" nagged the Speaker, his face gradually taking the shape of Richard Nixon on a lemon binge. "You there! With the sideburns! Quit squawking about and sit down!"

Dissenting murmurs rippled through the assembly.

"Here we go again."

"I can think of a few places he can stick that gavel."

"We would have been better off with the *real* Nixon . . . well, maybe not—but it's close."

"I am the duly appointed One In Charge, at least for the next few minutes, and I will have ORDER!" The Speaker's gavel—which was really nothing more than an ornament designed to be hung from the rearview mirrors of cars owned by judges who wished to make sure that anyone who missed the black robe *and* the "Oliver Wendell *Who*?!" bumper sticker was reminded that they were driving with someone most likely more important than they were— punctuated the end of the ultimatum with a frenzied succession of inert clonks. This inaudible hammering continued, increasing in exponential fury, until one of the backbencher's bladders—coerced into action through an apoplectic fit of hoots, woops, and snorts—decided that now was as good a time as any to redecorate the inside of its owner's chinos. The resulting trouser puddle—unmistakable, unbecoming, and moist—was the generally accepted signal to finally take a seat and get down to brass tacks. (Mind you, not because everyone was content that they had ruffled a suitable number of feathers and adequately stirred the gumbo—though they most certainly had—but more so due to the fact that the bar had been drunk dry.) This particular parliamentary procedural quirk, originally instituted to be the only "proper" way to conclude a Question Time counter-rebuttal, was just one of the many archaic customs grandfathered in from the long defunct and even less remembered little polity known as the British House of Commons. Though comically ineffective and barbarous by modern standards, pound for pound you'll be hard-pressed to find a body of government anywhere that could turn the allocation and administration of goods and services into more entertaining theater than those limey British hooligans.

"Now that you've all had your fun," sneered the Speaker, glancing longingly at his brand-new, yet-to-be-used driver, "we can finally get down to the business of the day. If there are no objections, I declare this session open."

He paused for a moment, and then began, "Now, on to the little matter concerning the end of my term. As has been tradition and law since the Beginning, the Speaker may only serve one term which, I don't have to remind you all, coincides with the beginning and end of the Universe. Let me just say that it has been an honor serving as the Speaker for this go round, and that I hold you all in the utmost esteem." This bald-faced lie might have been more believable were the Speaker not wearing Richard Nixon's face, but in any event it was the "right and proper" thing to say at The End Of It All.

A smattering of applause and a grumble of acceptance permeated the ranks. The Speaker *had* been a snooty, hoity-toity phlegm bag—*that* no one would or could deny; but he had been a capable administrator. His Universe had been, for the most part, a better-run affair than any in recent memory. Sure, there had been a few kerfuffles along the way—the dill-pickle scandal, some over-nepotistic appointments here and there, the Nixonian moues—but most of the real hot potatoes, proper nocuous opprobrium, had happened way back when the Universe was still expanding, and was more or less completely forgotten by now. Almost all of the black holes had been re-paved, dark matter had never been more enigmatic, and that whole business about that damned dead cat in the box had finally been put to rest. Definitively.

"Billy, the curtain, if you would," snapped the Speaker.

Behind him the entire front wall of the chamber, previously covered in red velvet, gave way to a panoramic viewing window. The clock above the window had reached ten seconds. 5 . . . 4 . . . 3 . . . 2 . . . and in that final second the Universe, which at that point resembled a deflating, softball-sized garbanzo bean, was observed by all present to collapse harmlessly onto itself with little more than a high pitched "pip" similar to the sound you get when you suck a Mack truck through a straw at eight billion times the speed of light.

The requisite unenthusiastic applause trickled around the room, and everyone turned back to the podium unimpressed, just in time to catch the tail end of the ex-Speaker's golf bag exit the chamber in a blur.

A bespectacled gentleman—ample around the waist, stout above the feet, and clumsy in the tongue—stepped forward. He glanced at his pocket watch, nervously adjusted the microphone and, being one of the more junior members of the assembly, began sweating.

Very few things are more imposing than a room filled with old men. There is just something unsettling about dealing with people who no longer care that their eyebrows have the consistency of a woolly mammoth. Facing them outside, although not advisable, gives you an outside shot; but within the walled confines of a room or chamber, survival is about as likely as having fun on a night out in Salt Lake City. As the youthfully challenged advance in age, they grow impervious to heat, each one turning up the thermostat every time he passes it. The lucky ones melt before the incessant barrages of "Is the heat on?!" and "Somebody better close that window!" cause their heads to implode like defective cinnamon rolls.

The thoroughly stout, amply perspirated gentleman cleared his throat, firing a projectile glottal salvo through the microphone. Percussive feedback yielded him the floor.

"P-P-P-Please, gentlemen. In ac-c-c-c-cordance with procedural by-laws, names w-w-w-will now be accepted into nomination for the new Speaker," stammered the poor fellow, woozy, having already lost six pounds.

The Speaker's office was of the highest prestige, charged with setting policy for and administering the Universe for one whole term—that being from The Bang, however "big" the Speaker had determined to be prudent at the front end, to the inevitable garbanzo bean at the back end. It was a position of unprecedented power and standing, but like most government jobs it was a "promotion" which involved doing boat-loads more work and requiring infinitely larger supplies of aspirin for only slightly more money than the standard job of an MP, which really only involved milling about and getting schlitzed while occasionally voting "yea" or "nay" on assorted motions or omnibus bills. As such, it was a position most people really didn't care to have. Who needed all that hassle when it was much easier to just sit back and guzzle down the bug juice like some freeloading Dead-head vagabond?

To be sure, there was the occasional up-and-comer, too young (comparatively) to realize that hard work and elbow grease were the domain of the lower classes, those who had the unfortunate disposition of having something to prove. These clueless dullards often made fine patsies for the brass to write in when no one was stupid enough to volunteer. And then there were those adept bureaucrats who understood that taking the Universe for a little joy-ride once around the cul-de-sac could really give you a significant leg up on the competition when looking to land that lucrative position in the private sector, no matter how much you had managed to muck everything up.

The previous Speaker, being a penny-pinching, nincompoop ape-brain, had skimped royally on just about every budgetary requirement. His greatest blunder, convincing himself that the Universe "really didn't need all this dust floating about, especially at this price"—this in direct contradiction to The Single, Primary, Universal, And Only Accepted Law For Governing The Construction Of A Universe: #1 You had better start with a big-ole bushel of dust or you can kiss the entire enterprise sayonara—has since surpassed coffee-flavored yogurt as the Worst Idea Ever. Needless to say the whole kit and caboodle got off the ground about as well as asbestos cigarettes. It did not, however, stop the man from procuring a cushy job on the board of directors of the third largest company around, the minute his Titanic of a term ended. He now spends his days eating money sandwiches.

"D-d-d-do we have any nominations, g-g-g-gentlemen?"

The silence that strangled the bustling chamber was akin to the one following an F-bomb that has conspicuously squirted out at a nunnery bake sale. Eyeballs ping-ponged this way and that as the members scanned the room for evidence of motion, all the time painstakingly endeavoring not to make any movement which might be considered complicit in indicating that one wished to speak. Nominations are like a high-stakes auction. Inadvertently scratch your nose or flatulate and, before you know it, you are stuck with a costly piece of garage-sale memorabilia that nobody else wanted.

Finally, an elderly statesman near the back stood up. "I think that everyone here knows who should be given the reins this time around."

The right side of the chamber nodded their heads in unison. Their universal grunt signaled acquiescence. The left side grumbled and glowered.

"There is only one man I can think of who has the passion, experience, and expertise to rudder this barge. He has served in the previous eleven administrations in every position of worth with distinction and competence. He's a family man, a company man, a righteous man, the candy man, a man's man, a *lady's* man, *and* a twelve handicap. Trustworthy, honest, above-board; a real straight-shooter. And did I mention he's bona fide?"

The right side became fizzy with excitement in their realization that such a qualified candidate was one of their native sons.

"*And* you will recall his outspoken opposition to that calamitous dust debacle a ways back."

This last statement had everyone, even on the left side, bobbing their heads in agreement.

"I nominate—"

And with that a handsome lion near the front stood up, his hand raised in humble acceptance. This gentleman was perfection, covered in chocolate, wrapped in hyperbole. He was slim and healthy, and he stood with impeccable posture. His tailored conservative-black suit emanated none of the stodginess often associated with tailored conservative-black suits; it was supplemented by a crisp white shirt with an open button where the necktie should have been. Every hair in his silver mane was present and accounted for. He had the look of a man who knew the menu better than the waiter.

"Hear, hear!" the calls rang out.

"I second the motion!"

"I third!"

"Do we need another second?"

"O-O-O-Order, gentlemen! The nomination is seconded and carried. Are there any other nominations?"

This sent the left side into a delirious flit. There was no one, if left up to any form of coherent discussion, who would be more qualified than such a pro-dust powerhouse. But a challenger was needed, fast, if not just to keep up appearances.

"Going once." The unrest was now palpable. "Going twice." A whole section in the back-left fainted in plenary. "Going three times. Appointed . . . that is unless there are any objections," he added, groping the left side of the chamber with a rummaging gaze. "Anyone who has any objections speak now or forever hold your peace."

The deafening silence that followed was interrupted by a snoring cannonade off the port side.

"Who s-s-s-said that? S-S-S-Speak up, please."

After some shifting around and even more smelling-salts, a man was spatulaed off the floor and propped up against the back wall. He was wearing a coon-skin cap and soiled red full-body long johns, the kind where the bottom flap can be unbuttoned to let the wearer evacuate his bowels without having to go through the arduous process of undressing. The key to this paragon of lavatorial conveni-ence is all in the order: One, open flap. Two, evacuate. By the look and smell of it, and by the flies, it appeared the man had on more than one occasion made his omelet without first cracking the eggs. Although he was not dead, his right arm was. Rigor mortis had clenched his hand around a rusty hip flask, and from a distance the substance on his face could only be accurately described as some permutation of beard and lunch. He spoke only in vowels and with an aroma reserved for outhouses and armpits.

The man next to him, politically savvy as he was, jumped.

"I nominate . . . uh . . . this guy."

"Hear, hear?" sheepishly bleated a man in the fourth row.

"I second the motion?" blurted another.

"I third?" questioned a third with all the conviction of French Toast.

"We don't need another second, do we?"

"The m-m-m-motion is seconded and carried. Would the two candidates make their way to the podium for the debate, please."

Any rational being from the planet Earth, employing the principle that objects in nature naturally make informed—and therefore the best—decisions based on rational examination of all possible outcomes and their consequences, and having compared the two candidates side by side, would have inevitably come to the conclusion that any competition between the two would be a complete farce and hence a waste of time, especially considering that the prize was complete control of the Universe. Even more especial with the dust fiasco fresh in everyone's salad. Any inkling of debate would have been prudently bypassed in favor of giving the most obviously over-qualified candidate the keys to the Chevy.

Anyone from anywhere else *besides* Earth would have given himself a mild stroke whooping around like a stoned hyena upon hearing that anyone in the Universe still actually subscribed to such a ludicrous line of thinking. Adam Smith thought like that. So did Karl Marx. They were both dolts—although both are still bestselling humor authors on Klom-phithiroo Prime.

"Knock knock."

"Who's there?"

"Bettersit."

"Bettersit who?"

"We had better sit down and think about this before we do something stupid." That one always cracks 'em up.

Farce is the natural state of all things, no matter how much dust there is wafting about. It is the life-blood of existence. Farce dribbles through every particle, anti-particle, quark, and quasitron like a Benny Hill punchline on amphetamines, brazenly tooting its kazoo and stealing rationale's lunch money every chance it gets. Anyone who believes otherwise need only mosey on down to any local, county, state, regional, federal, or cosmic legislature.

Being so, the farce that was the debate for the One In Charge commenced without so much as a woolly eyebrow raised in opposition.

The lion sauntered stately up to the podium to lay out the vision for *his* Universe. The speech that followed was the most eloquent, well-worded, comprehensive, best-structured, oratorical masterpiece ever uttered. Every word he used polled better than free money. Laid out were plans for a whole new manner of Universe, one in which there would be a chicken in every pot, a pot for everyone to piss in, and free pot for anyone who wanted it, all while abolish-ing pot-holes *and ironing*. The simple beauty of his method twanged the very heart-strings of every politician present. In one ambitious wallop, the ills that had given the Universe hemorrhoids since before gravity had been made mandatory would be amputated from its galactic derriere.

The opus came to its conclusion. Raucous applause erupted from the gallery. Hands were clapped bloody. And when the members on both the right *and* the left had finished mutilating their metacarpi into pulpy red stumps, they sat down, content in knowing that they had just witnessed history in the making. The silver hero gracefully bowed his head and receded to his chair, knowing his chance of winning was better than that of the Globetrotters'.

"O-O-O-Order, Gentlemen! And now for the re-b-b-b-buttal." All the MPs, having completely forgotten about the other speech, returned to their seats, rolling their eyes as if they were just forcefully made to watch the end-credits of a movie.

The challenger stood up, attempted to button his bottom, and managed to lurch in the general direction of the podium. Undaunted by following the most unfollowable of acts—mostly having to do with his having been passed out through its entirety and therefore unaware of the impossibly long odds he faced, or for that matter what his name was or where his left boot had gotten to—he opened his mouth in an attempt at verbal communication.

It is here, if you hear anyone who was there tell it, that this disheveled husk of a deplorable excuse for a life form articulated a counter-argument of political sublimity. Spoken aloud, the remark, so succinct and perfectly devoid of any meaning or relevance while simultaneously conveying the allusion of exactly the opposite, was the great white whale of inane political discourse. It was the gyroball of sound bites. The promised land:

"Fuck taxes!

"Yay puppies!

"This Bud's for you!"

In the subconscious depths of the cosmos, The Kazoo sounded, resonating every quantum particle in a key out-to-lunch in absurd reality.

"HEAR, HEAR!"

"AND HEAR!"

"A-A-A-All those in favor?"

"AYE!"

"Op-p-p-p-posed?"

". . ."

"Th-th-th-the ayes have it. Mr. Speaker, you may begin The Bang at your convenience—once you have finished your drink, of course. This session is c-c-c-closed."

Another bull's-eye. Hear, hear!

II

Code 19

"I'll get right on it, sir. Am I to assume that this mission is going to be . . . off the books, so to speak? Strictly hush-hush?"

"You've hit the donkey in the ass there, agent. As of this moment, I am the only other person who knows of this little operation. Let's keep it that way for the time being."

"What operation, sir?"

"That's the spirit. I knew you would be the right woman for the job. Get in there and rustle us up some intel. Find out who is still loyal to the cause down there and report back to me. Get in. Get out. Inconspicuous as water chestnuts in an off-Broadway salad."

"So . . . no wings then, sir?"

"No wings. We're not dealing with a bunch of shepherds anymore."

• • •

CODE 19. Why, oh *why*, did it have to be a nineteen? There were umpteen other codes which could, at any given time, serve as the impetus to be called into the Boss's office. Code 3: the Boss needs some coffee. That one was a cakewalk. Code 112: duplicate-triplecate discrepancy interrogation. Dicey—yes. Life threatening—no. Code 492: Heimlich maneuver requested—urgently. Thrust in and up. It took longer to say than to execute. Any one of them was better than the sinister one-niner.

Code 19 was rarely, if ever, used. Only the most wizened of stalwart company codgers could even recall it being implemented at all. Most employees didn't even know it existed. It was a mythic piece of corporate hogwash, a cautionary yarn spun by section leaders to rookie employees during training to scare them into drinking the company Kool-aid and overlooking the substandard dental coverage. Put simply, a Code 19 was a root canal, a trip to the principal's office, and your mother-in-law all furled into one epically heinous egg roll: It was bad news.

The only time Code 19 was evoked was when something somewhere had gone completely, utterly, incomprehensibly wrong. Not the *Billy fudged the numbers on his paperwork and now we've run out of red ink in which to finish writing the number at the bottom of the quarterly report* wrong, or even the *Does bankruptcy make you sterile?* wrong, but the *Something is so über-FUBAR that the Big Boss Man himself is taking point on this one and just go on and venture a guess as to who he has fingered to spearhead the cleanup operation* wrong. The proverbial shit has hit—smashed into, rather—other proverbial mega-shit in the proverbial Superconducting Shit Super Collider. You can forget about finding that shifty little Higgs Bozo-ma-thingy, not to mention that long weekend you were looking forward to.

Employee number 3905-6Z Θ is painfully aware of the ramifications of a Code 19 as she crosses the threshold into the Boss's office. She has been in here before—many times actually, usually to receive some sort of commendation, pat on the back, or 'at-a-girl on account of the bang-up job she has been doing—but this time the atmosphere is decidedly more vexing and thorny. There is a hint of flammability in the air, a summer barbecue with all propane and no burger. The office is in strobe, the only light intermittently pulsing out of a red wall panel ominously blinking "CODE 19" above the Boss's desk. Sitting behind a heavy oak fuselage in an absurdly oversized wingback chair with his hands folded neatly on the desk in front of him, the Boss beckons her in. His face is in shadow—a bullet dodged for sure. Were his mirth-coagulating scowl clearly visible, something would have to give. More than likely it would have been the ligaments in employee number 3905-6Z Θ's knees.

"Come in, agent."

"Yes, sir." She advances deeper into the bowels of the crypt, the Boss increasing incrementally in size as his image alternates from darkness to Code 19 red with each cyclical spasm of the wall panel. By the time she reaches the desk, he has attained normal Boss size.

He breathes audibly for a few moments, expelling the last remnants of amusement from his body, then decides that this conversation should be done on his feet. You can't be *that* angry when you're sitting down. He stands up slowly and deliberately, as if easing out of an all-you-can-eat coma at the Old Country Buffet, and turns to face the window behind the desk, leaving employee number 3905-6Z Θ to converse with his backside.

"We have a problem, agent," he begins.

"Yes, sir."

"I need you to fix it."

"Right, sir."

"Fast."

"Of course, sir." Employee number 3905-6Z Θ has not gotten to be one of the rising stars in the Company by tittering away like a Tagalong vendor. When dealing with any of the higher-ups the best thing to do is go Marine-style. No frills. No excess verbiage. Just straight-up, home-cooked affirmatives peppered with more "sirs" than a Westminster key party.

"Take a look at this." He hands her a small orange brochure.

It takes her less than two seconds to read it in its entirety. "Is this what I think it is, sir?"

"If you think it's the financial equivalent of a quantum singularity, sucking money from this company—from *me*—like a vampire leach divorcee, then yes it is."

"Do we know who, sir?"

"Agent Churlborough, section eighty-one. He's gone rogue." A *rogue* agent, doling out orange brochures like these—this is even worse than she imagined. "You know what to do, agent."

"Yes, sir."

"I need you over in eighty-one yesterday. Get on top of this."

III

THE MAN IN BLACK

"Do you think he's bluffing?"

"He could be."

"So how do I tell if he's bluffing?"

"You'll know."

"Yeah, but how?"

"When his cards are worse than yours."

"But I can't see his cards. How do I get him to show them?"

"You might try bluffing."

"All right, let's give that a go . . . Uh, Karl?"

"Yeah?"

"What's bluffing?"

• • •

THE FIRST thing that entered Stan's field of vision was the set of cards organized neatly in his hand. They had not yet come into focus, but Stan was reasonably sure they were playing cards—the ones composed of one-eyed jacks, suicide kings, those maniacal eights, and the like. Beyond them, the silhouette of a man was the only thing visible through the blinding fog that had gradually aggregated in the cramped back room. The acrid cloud levitated thick and ominous in the air like pipe-organ music. Stan could feel it seeping in through his eyeballs. The pile of cigarette butts stacked in front of him formed a stout defense against any frontal attack and reminded his lungs who wore the pants in the relationship.

A cursory sweep of his immediate surroundings turned up very little except for the fact that he wasn't wearing any pants. It appeared to Stan that he had gotten himself involved in some sort of game of chance. Whether or not this also entailed some derivation of a smoking competition was up in the air, being cured like beef jerky. He was seated at a large round table along with seven other seats, only one of which was at present peopled. Occupying the Arthurian position directly across from him was a man who lacked the gravitas—and posture—to be the legendary king of ole Camelot. Stan ruled out Lancelot, as well—much too old and serrated. He wore a Basset hound for a face, and his jaw cantilevered out past his nose like over-ambitious decking. Stan ball-parked his age at a hundred and ten. Instead of breathing, the man manually lassoed wild chunks of air with his tongue, swallowed them raw without chewing, and then brought them back up with a ramshackle system of wheezing winches and sputtering pulleys. He came pre-dressed for his funeral, wearing black from head to toe except for a white collar. In the center of the table was a steaming pile of unadulterated wealth. It was difficult to see through the haze, but Stan could make out a jungley assortment of chips, cash, coins, watches, keys, and treasury bonds. He spotted his left trouser cuff trying fruitlessly to escape from under the weight of a framed Joe DiMaggio rookie card with a stack of diamond-studded caviar balanced on top. That was at least one mystery solved. Now, if he could only figure out who this wheezing menace was and what exactly he was doing here, he would be well on his way to recalling his middle name.

Stan tried to piece together the events of the evening that had led him to this precarious position. He petitioned his brain but the response was broadcast through the speaker of a drive-thru window. He sifted through the static: He had started out the evening at the bar with Karl; they had a drink. The rest was blank. He cursed himself above his breath for being, yet again, in such an unfriendly spot with yet another hostile breeze whistling through his boxer shorts.

Every time Stan decided to have a drink, he invariably decided that it wouldn't be a bad idea to have a few dozen more. This was not because Stan was an alcoholic, but rather because he was a history buff. He found it much more nostalgic to drink as would a great hero of yesteryear, instead of the namby-pamby, lily-livered wusses of the day. If Alexander the Great and Benjamin Franklin could drink until slavery was legal, then why not he? He imbibed in the Churchillian method—with unbridled reckless abandon and captivating stump speeches. When the dust mercifully settled, Stan would come to—broke, bleeding, and befuddled—with his mouth tasting like flambeed camel droppings. Tonight was no different, except for the fact that he knew where his pants were—a problem Churchill could never seem to solve. *If only Karl were here,* he lamented inwardly. *Karl can always remember at least twenty percent of what has happened.*

"Pssst. Stan." A finger materialized out of a swirling plume and tapped Stan on the shoulder. It was Karl.

"Karl! Where have you been? I'm dying over here!"

"What are you talking about? I've been sitting right next to you, right here, for the last seven hours!"

"Well . . . sorry. I didn't see you there with all this smoke."

After letting his eyes adjust it became apparent that Karl was, in fact, sitting not two feet away from him.

• • •

Knuckles Artichoke Rent-a-car Livingston—Karl—was an undulating walrus of a man who had retired to live on the Moon because the genes he and a long line of Livingstons lugged around were duds—not all of them, of course, just the ones responsible for the Livingston family chicken legs. His forefathers had survived only through carefully keeping everything above their waists in manageable proportion to their paltry lower appendages. This was done through scrupulous genetic screening of any and all possible mates. Anyone with a body mass index over 23.5 didn't make the cut. The Livingstons, mind you, were not bigots; many of their friends were glandular and slovenly—but when it came to reproduction, fatties could not be tolerated. The resulting offspring would possess the structural stability of a balsa-wood buttress.

Karl's father, Hambone, being the rebel that he was, did not heed the advice of his kin. He had lost all his money investing in Mexico. When the country went belly up, he was left destitute with nothing but a raggedy sombrero and a handful of pesos. The pesos were enough to buy a bottle of tequila—which is what he did. He awoke the next morning with a heavy-metal concert in his head, a whale in his arms, and a wedding ring on his finger. The whale was Karl's mother. She had been knocked up on that very first night.

Any apprehensions Hambone had about the ramifications of inviting such unwieldy genetic material in for supper instantly evaporated the moment he saw his new wife's bank statement. She was drowning in wealth. Hambone had found his sugar mama.

Unfortunately for Karl, he inherited his mother's leviathan torso and his father's legs. His disproportionality was magnified many times over by his cushy upbringing. The only time he ever lifted a finger to do anything constructive—and then only when the feeding servants had retired for the evening—was to stuff his face with bon-bons and banana splits. Boy, did he love banana splits. In the end, walking around in regular Earth gravity on his laughably inadequate chicken legs had become such a chore that he just packed everything up and hightailed it to the one-sixth gravity haven of the Moon.

On the Moon his amoeba frame buoyed around the room with all the grace of an ice barge, leaving spilled drinks, small furniture, and dirty looks in his ever-swelling wake. His very own personal gravity well served to keep an endless supply of cocktails, cigarette smoke, and dirty jokes orbiting his planetary midriff. At the moment he was stooped comically atop a footstool which, inexplicably, was not showing signs of buckling under the strain of supporting his colossal chassis. Even in one-sixth gravity, the fact that the stool had not collapsed stood as a miraculous testament to its superb craftsmanship. Incidentally, it was also the karmic prison for the soul of a man who had stolen candy from babies. He got a bum rap, if you ask me. The real crime was giving candy to a baby in the first place. Who does that?

Dressed head to toe in shag denim, the height of fashion since the Monday before last, he resembled a Canadian opera singer on the juice. He had the head of a six-year-old, made to appear even smaller when compared with his commodious frame. No discernible chin or, for that matter, jaw could be identified, having been obscured by a marshmallowy cluster of jowls that slung off his cheekbones like love handles on a mashed-potatoes-and-cashew diet. Whether or not he possessed a neck was the subject of much speculation. With the excess bulk around his face tucked with care and precision just a little too neatly into his buttoned collar, his oxygen-depleted face fashionably matched the color of his denim apparel.

Despite his pressed shirt and expensive shag suit, the overly tangible nature of his build prevented his clothes from fitting properly and relegated his first impressions to those of a much less-monied citizen. He was all wide angles without a corner to be found, a fleshy Escher. Trying to follow his silhouette played Catch 22 with your eyeballs as you invariably ended up where you started without knowing how you got there and feeling cheated for having made the attempt.

Karl never spoke; he bombarded. A conversational pugilist, Karl lectured in bombastic prose, punctuating argumentative jabs with hooks of expensive whiskey, lobbing great oratorical haymakers at whatever poor soul had the misfortune of sitting next to him. His voice carried through any medium with impunity. A man of conviction, he was seldom mistaken and never wrong—a republican—one of a dying breed long lost to the annals of American political history, who disdained homosexuals, free-loaders, and ice dancers. He was a self-made man who, having lifted himself up by the bejeweled bootstraps provided by his obscenely rich mother, used every opportunity in life to stand proudly on the shoulders of the little guy and rain antipathy down upon him from his summer-home balcony.

His friends found him detestable, and everyone else loathed the mere idea of mentioning his name. He was the life of the party.

• • •

"So what am I doing, and who is he?" inquired Stan, pivoting his eyes toward his geriatric foe.

"You're playing poker."

"Poker?"

"Poker. Five card stud."

"But I don't know how to play poker!"

"Yes, you do. At least you have known how to play for the last seven hours. You have been cleaning up, too. The only guy left at the table is him there," said Karl, pushing aside a curtain of smoke like heavy drapery and leaning sideways to allow Stan a better look.

"Who's he?"

"They call him 'The Padre.' Real nasty fellow."

"He doesn't look so tough," lied Stan.

"You should see him without the smoke." Karl shuddered.

"Wait—I'm winning?" reconfirmed Stan incredulously. It didn't seem possible. Stan never won at anything—ever.

"Yeah, you're winning. If you play this hand right you could take home the whole pot!"

As this last sentence reverberated between his ears, Stan unconsciously remembered why he never gambled. Consciously, he just couldn't help himself. "I bet it all!"

Gasps could be heard emanating from the smoky void that surrounded everything five feet outside the table. Evidently, they were not alone.

"But you only have four cards!" objected Karl.

Stan brushed him aside. This was no time for prudence. This was a time for action—pure, unfiltered stupidity. That is always the best way to keep everyone on their heels *and* their toes. Try going anywhere like that. I dare you.

"Five cards are for hairdressers and bathroom attendants!" declared Stan, soap-boxing on his chair. "I'll take these four beauties here over any five you got, Padre." As he taunted the old man with the one-eyebrow shuffle, the thought occurred to him that he may have made a small error in calculation by not ever bothering to take notice of what cards he actually held in his hand.

The man they called "The Padre" made a smile-like gesture—or at least the closest thing he could hope for as he was trying to make it out of a cantilevered Basset hound. One thing was for sure: Stan's high-flying circus act bluff had not scared him in the least. His face evened out, though, after counting his remaining chips.

Karl picked up on his cue. "Looks like you're a little short there, gramps," he said, trying to form his doughy cheeks into a smirk.

Then the old man did something he hadn't done all night. He spoke.

"Not so fast, sonny," he rasped. His voice sounded like it had been churned out of rancid butter. He reached into his back pocket and pulled out a piece of paper. It was the deed to his home. He adhered it to the side of the heap in the center of the table with a wad of caviar, then sneered at Stan. "Full boat! Kings over queens!" cackled The Padre as he cracked the cards down.

Stan was heartbroken. He had no idea what a "full boat" was, but judging from the reaction of the bodiless voices from beyond the cancerous smog, the distance he guesstimated Karl's jaw had dropped under his pillowy dermis, and the verve with which The Padre was now doing a river-dance jig, he surmised that it was most likely better than the complete garbage he more than likely had.

He picked up his hand and studied its contents intently. It was times like this when he really wished that he knew the first thing about playing poker. He turned the cards upside down to see if that would make things better. No help at all.

"Well . . .?" prompted Karl. Stan gave him an aloof shoulder shrug.

"What does an 'A' mean?" he asked.

"That's an ace."

"Are aces good?"

"They can be. Why?"

"Cuz that's all I have. Four A's."

IV

The Woman in White

"And good luck to all our contestants here in round one. We'll start with you, Robert."

"Let's try 'Wow! I Didn't See That Coming' for 300, please."

"Reported to be 'all in a huff over not getting invited to the bread-buttering competition,' he stormed into the Senate chamber to let everyone know just how hurt he was to be left out of the fun and to demand he be given a knife, too."

"Who is Julius Caesar?"

"Correct."

"'Wow!' for 400, please."

"This was inadvertently discovered when a Swiss chemist decided that working with strange and exotic chemicals all morning did not constitute a good enough reason to wash your hands before munching down a bologna sandwich."

"What is LSD?"

"Correct."

"'Wow!' for 500, please."

"Display one of these to make everyone safer."

"What is an automatic rifle?"

• • •

TUESDAYS WERE always the worst.

The traffic on Aldrin Avenue had petrified. The only saving grace was that today happened to fall somewhere in between one of the intermittent lunar nights that gave the "dark side" of the Moon a two-week reprieve from the sun's ovening properties. If this traffic jam had been during the day, the heat would have been unbearable. The number 32 bus had meandered through the west side of town along Sea of Tranquility Two Park, looped around the observatory, and was now making its weekly futile advance down Buzz A. Ave.

Gumballs Miller took the number 32 almost every day. He knew the regular passengers better than the back of the lenses on the overtly unstylish, horn-rimmed bi-focals he had defiantly worn daily for the last forty-seven years. Why should he buy a new pair of glasses when these still got the job done perfectly fine? Being one of the younger members of the regular 32 crowd, Gumballs always made his nest near the back, sparing the more elderly patrons the extra fifteen feet of bus-aisle gauntlet. Some of those fogies moved slower than bureaucratic apathy. They could put the bus behind schedule.

Gumballs was eighty-nine years young.

In the seat next to him was his good friend, Pumpernickel. He was napping, as usual. Moving about really took it out of Pumps. Across the aisle, Mrs. Cuthbert and her feminine cohorts were on the way home from their weekly Tuesday afternoon assembly at the Crocheter's Guild. She was the treasurer because of her knack for numbers. She couldn't, of course, keep a single one of them in her head longer than a goldfish could, but she *was* fastidious about writing them all down.

"Lovely day, *Mizz* Cuthbert, isn't it?" charmed Gumby. He had a reputation as a bit of a lady's man.

"Who are you?!" she goldfished back.

Moving on, Gumballs tested himself on the names of the passengers, one by one, as they aged down the narrow lane in front of him. Any reason to flex the ole memory muscle. There was Parsley Grant, who was still spry at a hundred and two, with his wife, who was not. In front of them was Happenstance Griswald, taking up his usual two seats, one for Hap and one for his colostomy bag. Tuesdays were buffet day down at the bingo hall. He spotted the Diedermeyer triplets a ways further up. Just last week all three had placed in the annual uneven bars competition in the 125–140 age class. Next year they would be moving up to heavy-age. They might as well hand out the trophies now and get it over with. Finally, in the very front sat the matriarch of the bus, Bermuda Coughlin. At a hundred and seventy-five years of age, she was one of the oldest living souls on the entire Moon. She had gotten on at the clinic having just received her sixth hip implant only to find the incorrigible Clavicle Hunt in her seat. She quickly dispatched him with a banshee nag. Reluctantly, he sulked to the back of the bus. At seventy-six, Clav was too young to know any better.

It was days like these, when the bus was packed tighter than country-singing blue jeans, when Gumballs really missed his car. Back on Earth he had paraded stately around town in his emerald-green Cadillac Coupe de Ville, but living on the Moon he wasn't allowed to drive it anymore. No one was allowed to drive on the Moon—except for the bus drivers. It was a prudent move. They had allowed people to drive themselves around once, and it had been an unmitigated disaster. The reason for this was that eighty-three percent of the Moon's population was over seventy-five years old. No one wanted them on the road. Of the remaining seventeen percent, the majority was comprised of longshoremen, who made sure the inordinate quantities of pharmaceuticals and medicinal creams made their way efficiently through the space ports and into the arthritic hands of the slowly withering population. No one wanted them on the road, either. The rest was topped off with the nurses, doctors, and health-care workers necessary to keep the old people paying property taxes, and to fix up the longshoremen after they had broken their falling-down-drunk faces on each other's free-swinging-drunk fists. And, of course, the bus drivers.

This seemingly peculiar allocation of the overly aged was not a result of the Moon being taken over by the Japanese. It was all gravity's fault. When Earthlings first began venturing into space on a commercial level, the Moon had been a trendy getaway for rich debutantes and their trophy partners. They liked coupling in one-sixth gravity. The luster on this Moon lust tarnished quickly, though, when it became apparent that any prolonged vacationing in the low-gravity environment rendered the bones more brittle than French hospitality, making any return to Earth impossible—or at the very least, debilitatingly painful. Most everyone decided to just stay on Earth and do it the old-fashioned way, at six times the exertion.

The one upside to the Moon's gravity shortfall was that it made the perfect repository for all Earth's unwanted old people. No longer did people have to throw out or euthanize their money-sieve relatives once they had matured past their expiration dates. One-sixth gravity meant one sixth the drag on pendulous faces and sagging breasts, five times less effort to get up out of bed in the morning, and five times less coaxing needed to rouse the old battle veteran when the missus had a hankerin' for the good stuff. Since everyone's hips were on the verge of shattering anyhow, the little matter of bone density wasn't really an issue. Most important, the distance from the Earth to the Moon was just far enough to give everyone the perfect excuse not to visit every other weekend, but not so far as to put one out too much when the eventual quality time became mandatory. Like Florida, only better. Win, win.

Still, Gumballs would have given his good eye for his Cadillac right about now.

The bus pulled up to the stop out in front of McPhereson's Excitement Center. The queue extended all the way to the corner and dog-legged around the building, out of sight. For all anyone knew, the line continued on to infinity. Gumballs groaned.

McPhereson's was one of the reasons the number 32 was such a popular transportation destination. It was the most popular recreational retreat in town, mostly due to the fact that it played *Jeopardy* nonstop on big-screen TVs throughout the sprawling complex, which included a par-three golf course, a bingo bar, and a pharmacy, peppered with state-of-the-art shuffle-board courts and indoor-outdoor rest-stop recliners.

Tuesdays were the perfect storm. The golf course's Tuesday afternoon two-dollar price reduction, as well as concurrent meetings at the Crocheter's Guild and the When I Was Your Age Foundation, all ended simultaneously. The golfers, crocheters, and bitter nostalgics mobbed the bus stops only to find an already substantial mass of geriatric hubbub waiting for the daily "Up All Night" three-percent bus-ticket discount to kick in—all at four p.m. With lights out at 5:30, the transit authority had little choice but to increase the number of buses on route 32 to the point where it clogged up the municipal arteries worse than a weekend at the county fair.

"Hey, Pumps," jabbed Gumballs as he elbowed his best friend in the ribs, "get a load o' these guys." He motioned to the gaggle of golfers lumbering onto the bus, straining their eyes, as they did for their errant drives, to locate a non-existent open seat. "If they think I'm gonna give up my seat just because they got a couple a years on me, they got another thing coming."

Pumpernickel awoke apoplectic. "What is the Battle of Waterloo!"

"Oh wake up, will you? Something is about to go down." Gumball's instincts as a retired riot police were telling him to be on the alert. It was quarter past four and no one had eaten dinner yet. This could be an explosive situation.

The chieftain of the golfing clan took the lead, eyeballing the unwilling passengers spitefully as they silently refused his implied request for posterior relief by falling asleep. Once you hit eighty you didn't even have to fake it anymore. Eventually he came to Gumballs.

"Perty nice lookin' seat ye' got there, sonny. Hows about ye' let an ole man take a load off, eh? M'dogs are a barkin' some'n fierce," drawled the golfer, clearly exaggerating his elder-speak.

"Old man, my keister!" retorted Gumballs. "You ain't even pushin' triple digits, kiddo. Don't' give me this 'sonny' song and dance. Just move yourself right along. Me and Pumps here ain't budgin'. Isn't that right, Pumps?"

Pumps gave an obstinate snore.

"Isn't that right, Pumps?" he repeated with another prod to the ribs.

"What is Rubidium!"

All the cinnamon and sugar drained from the golfer's expression. He reached for his putter.

"I wasn't askin'. I was tellin'. Me and the boys here just finished hoofin' around the links for the last three and half hours. Now, we're gonna take those seats. And if you know what's good for you, you'll get up right now and move on down to the back of the bus." The men behind him pulled out their golf ball retrievers to show that they meant business.

"Now hold up just a second there, sir," whimpered Pumpernickel. "Ole Gumby, he didn't mean anything by—"

"The hell I didn't!" shouted Gumballs as he stood to make his challenge. "I'll be damned if I'm gonna give up my seat to a bunch of *duffers!*" This last insult really buried itself in the golfer's bunker. His face turned the color of a lateral water hazard.

By this time, every other passenger on the bus had been woken up by all the posturing. Every eye was now wallpapered to the two men, face to face, in the center of the bus. The smart money was on the guy with the putter: better reach. Gumballs did have his police background to fall back on, but he had retired over thirty years ago. A melee was set to ensue when more advanced celestial powers intervened.

Moments before the two men came to blows, they were halted by an ultra-low-frequency burping sound. This resonant tremor briefly led Gumballs to believe that someone had had a sub-woofer for lunch, but the notion quickly dissipated when a plume of black gelatinous pudding materialized out of the nothingness occupying the space betwixt the combatants. It hovered a few feet above the ground for a second, bloated as a pompous jackass, before collapsing in on itself like French courage soup. Three things then followed in quick succession: the staccato *pop-crunch-fluffle-thud* made when someone sits on a king-sized bag of unopened Funyuns, a puff of confetti and party streamers, and the manifestation of a blond bombshell.

Gumballs fished the confetti out of his gawking mouth and redid his double-take. An arm's length in front of him stood a stunning blond woman. She was dressed incandescently in pure alabaster business attire—jacket, blouse, skirt, shoulder bag—all glowing as white as the Founding Fathers. She was unsullied business acumen personified, except for the fact that she was wearing thick, handmade, leather moccasins. To be sure, they looked to be the epitome of comfort, but they just didn't jive with the rest of her ensemble.

"Oof," she exhaled as she hula-hooped her head around her neck and stretched skyward as if she had just rolled out of the right side of bed. "Is it just me or does that actually get *more* jarring every time you do it?"

Gumballs tried to tell his shocked brain to go ahead and blink. It was no use.

"Ooh, is someone sitting there?" she asked innocently, pointing to the seat Gumballs had just vacated. He managed to make a gentlemanly gesture in the general direction of his seat. "Oh, thank you so much," she said as she slid in gracefully. "I tell you, my dogs are really barking." She took off one of the moccasins and began to message her foot. That puppy must have really been howling; she was kneading her insole like devitalized Play-doh.

"Coming up on 7th and Aldrin," crackled the bus driver's voice over the loudspeaker.

"Hey, I think this is my stop," panicked the woman. "Do you mind holding this for a second?" It was not a request so much as a trivial demand made by a beautiful woman to the nearest available man knowing he would bend over backwards to fulfill it. Gumballs, dumbfounded and entranced, accepted the moccasin as she rifled through her shoulder bag and pulled out a map.

"7th and Aldrin—yep, this is me. Thanks," she said as she swiped the moccasin from his grasp. In one adroit motion she shimmied it onto her foot while standing up, simultaneously giving Gumballs a peck on the cheek for his troubles. He melted into teenage butter. The sea of knickered plaid parted before her, making sure to lift their golf ball retrievers out of the way. She exited the bus, checked her map, then headed down 7th Street and out of view. Gumballs watched every mystifying step—in love.

The thank-you peck still warm on his cheek, Gumballs felt more at peace than he ever had in his life. It was a good thing, too, because it was the last feeling he would ever have in his life. Lucky, considering the extensive hodgepodge of other feelings he could have been experiencing. His good friend Pumpernickel's last feeling, for example, was one of seething annoyance as he was awakened, he believed for the third time, from a pleasant dream starring Alex Trebek XIV by a poke in the ribs from his good friend Gumballs. He was wrong, though. The poke in his ribs was actually from a malfunctioning hover freighter, carrying eighty-two tons of emergency Metamucil rations, T-boning the number 32 bus from the sky like a bolt from Thor's hammer.

Bermuda Coughlin was the only survivor. She used her new hip and governor's spot at the front of the bus to dive out at the last second.

V

WHAT'S IN A NAME

"*Why do you drink so much?*"

"*Because it's there.*"

"*Goddamn it, Stan! I'm not talking about Mt. Everest. I'm talking about your goddamned life!*"

"*Appalling, sister, that you would take the Lord's name in vain. And in front of a man of the cloth, no less.*"

"*Oh, come off it. You're not even a priest. Don't be such an asshole.*"

"*Then how do you explain the church, goddamn it?*"

• • •

AFTER COLLECTING his winnings and waiting two hours for the smoke to clear to the point where an exit could be located, Stan and Karl promptly commandeered a parade float, headed back to the bar, and ordered the requisite two-dozen celebratory drinks—naturally paid for by Stan. He was loaded. He then ordered two-dozen drinks for everyone else at the bar. Not realizing that, at 9:45 in the morning, there was no one else at the bar until it was too late, he and Karl were forced to drink up the slack. Following that two-for-a-party-of-fifty, Stan decided to invest the remainder of his winnings, in entirety, into child-proof baby rattles. All his money evaporated into the artificial Moon air like a NASA grant. Penniless and hung over, Stan was left to beg on the streets like a daytime TV actor. Only after preparing himself to play the part of a down-to-his-last-can-of-beans vagrant by pulling his pockets inside out to demonstrate to any would-be upstart philanthropists that he didn't have any money squirreled away about his person, did he find the deed to The Padre's home. The caviar had dried it to the inside of his pocket. Thanking the Omniscient Shield Maidens of Valhalla for his good fortune, Stan made a beeline for his only possession: a church.

Hunkered down at the end of a desolate stretch of 7th Street, in between a dilapidated mom-and-pop delicatessen renowned for its Mooned ham and a vacant lot which doubled as a trash heap, Stan found his house of prayer. It was the worst church he had ever seen. It was the only church he had ever seen, but it was still, by far, the worst. The building and all of its accoutrements were the cheerless color of an elephant's behind, its only flourish a single, sad-sack steeple used to house dead birds. All the stained-glass windows had been traded for air cavities, and the entire structure leaned to the left like a bohemian poet. A sign above the front door read "House of God – Tread Lightly."

Stan had no way of knowing that this ramshackle little cathedral was, in fact, the only remaining church left—on the Moon or anywhere. Churches were an endangered species, you see. You could scour the far reaches of the Universe with a magnifying comb and you would still never come across another church. This was the last one. Just looking at it, Stan thought it was a good bet a stiff breeze would dodo-bird his new home into extinction like the Big Bad Bulldozer—a better bet, at least, than baby-proof rattles.

• • •

There was a time when churches littered the landscape of Earth—and the Moon. They had been the centers of commerce and learning for centuries. After that they had been the inhibitors of commerce and learning for centuries, but there were still a great many of them. Everywhere people went they built churches, first as great testaments to the skill and will of Man, and at the end as a way to embezzle money tax free.

The church fad had come abruptly to an end, though, when just about everyone on the planet converted to the brand new, shiny religion of the day—Chadism—at the beginning of the 22nd century. The ironically named Church of Chad didn't require its followers to build churches. It also didn't require them to gather for mindless weekly get-togethers, read ambiguous manuals, or jump through endless ecclesiastical hoops like trained house pets to attain spiritual rewards. It had only one rule—really just a guideline. The only tenet of the Church of Chad had been penned by its founder, Chadwick Churlborough, after finishing a stint in the Congo River Basin researching bonobos. The Chadics write this rule on all their brochures and claim that all those who follow it will be granted induction into Valhalla. The brochures are small, single-sheet, and orange, and the only thing written on them is this:

Just have sex as much as and with whomever you like!

Faced with the choice of being sauteed in Eternal Hell for contemplating the idea of masturbation, or using sex as the principle greeting, farewell, conflict resolver, stress reducer, secret ingredient, and standard recreational activity of everyday life, just about everyone jumped over to Chadism double-quick pronto.

The results of the Great Chadic Conversion were re-markable. First off, it concentrated most of the heavy lifting—day to day running of the society-wise—into the hands of the females. This by itself made everything run a whole lot smoother and delightfully more fragrant. Second, the world's population, which at that particular moment in history was having a difficult time squeezing into its global muu-muu without the aid of some creative stretching exercises, melted effortlessly into equilibrium as everyone who was a homosexual, which turned out to be just about the entire population, was freed up to have the homosex they had been longing to have instead of the baby-making kind they had been feigning interest in. A few straggling *old* church-going holdovers objected to everyone having relations with the people they wanted to have them with on account of it "just wasn't natural" until somebody posed a question to them:

"Hey, do you know what this is?"

"Of course I know what that is. Everyone knows what that is. It's one of those developmental toys given to every toddler on the planet."

"Right. So would you mind telling me what *this* is, then?"

"That's a round peg."

"And where does the round peg go?"

"Well, the round peg goes in the round hole. Naturally."

"Naturally. So tell me one more thing: If the Big Guy wasn't keen on homosexuality, why didn't He make assholes square?"

That settled the matter and glitter became a standard table condiment.

A handful of sore losers clung to the old ways like sanctimonious sloths. They were unhappy about all the glitter getting into their soup and even less thrilled about having to swap chromosomes with people they had no interest in swapping them with. They were quite the discontented bunch. In protest, they led a march on Washington DC, capital of the United States back then. Hundreds of thousands of people showed up for the event. Only sixteen of them stuck around for the march after they realized it wasn't another gay-pride parade. Able to read the writing on the wall, "The Faithful 16," as they had taken to calling themselves, packed up all their churches, Christmas trees, and sexual frustration onto a rickety old space barge rechristened *The Mayflower* and set off into an uncharted galaxy to practice their intolerance in peace. They tried to bring two of every animal along, but quickly found out there wasn't nearly enough space on the cramped space barge *Mayflower*. They had to settle instead for a pair of hamsters named Sodom and Gomorrah, and a three-legged armadillo called Phil.

• • •

Stan knew all of this well because Stan was an historian. Like his church, he was also the last of his kind. It wasn't that people thought that there wasn't any value in understanding what those who had gone before had done, how they had lived. It was because there just wasn't any money in it. And everyone knows: *If you can't make money doing it, then it's not worth being done.* Stan had known this when he decided to become a history major, but he was afraid of numbers and his first choice, Poli Sci, had already been filled to capacity by upperclassmen who liked college but didn't want to do anything especially stressful. The author of this book was someone like that.

The only thing Stan knew about running a church was that he didn't know how to do it. He didn't know the difference between a tabernacle and a quiche Lorraine. He *did* know about history, but that wouldn't help him make any money. Other than history, the only thing that Stan knew anything at all about was booze. He took the next logical step: He would turn his church into a bar and everything would be hunky-dory.

There was one problem, though.

Churches make the worst bars. In fact, churches are nearly impossible to renovate into any building where mirth and amusement are the principle modus operandi. You might be able to pull off a morgue or an Accounting 101 lecture hall, but that's about it. It's because of the atmosphere. The oxygen is lousy.

Churches are filled with antique, dour oxygen—as opposed to the regular ole peppy stuff you and I chuff down on our evening constitutionals. No one quite knows why, but the best guesses put the blame on all of the singing—or rather, imitation singing—that goes on. Songs are meant to bubble out of the soul like frothy, melodic goodness. Instead, what you get at church is that droning, vacuum-cleaner-type harmony only attainable by indirectly forcing entire congregations of unwitting drowsy-eyed parishioners to expectorate all eight lobotomizingly dull verses of "O' Ye Wretched Sinner Be Damned and Hell-Bound" first thing on a Sunday morning. With the question *If Sunday is supposed to be the day of rest then why in God's name can't I sleep in?*

bopping around in the back of everyone's head and their hangovers resonating fresh and crispy in the front and back and top and bottom and sides of their brain, malcontent hovers in the air on wisps of pungent frankincense. When this Sunday morning angst bonds with verse five, you get the chain reaction that produces the shoddy oxygen.

Once inhaled, this lugubrious chemical compound slithers its way to the capillaries around the fun receptors in the brain and burrows in like a hibernating hippie on a distant cousin's couch. It consumes all of the dopamine while everyone else is at work, leaving only discarded pizza boxes and unpaid long-distance phone bills. This is why it is impossible to smile or stay awake at church. The pizza boxes are clogging up the works.

And once that church oxygen seeps into the carpet in the aisles, and into the hymnals, and into the pews and the pores in the stained glass windows, it can be a real bitch to get out. The only way to rid your church of the contamination is through a labor-intensive process of re-jubilation. The first step involves endless hours of senior-calisthenics classes. Old people act as astonishingly efficient air scrubbers. Due to their advanced age, the majority of their fun receptors have already been renovated, through the body's natural hoarding enzymes, into attic space, packed to the gills with all the neural kitsch one accrues over extended living. Once inhaled, the church oxygen finds there is nowhere to nestle in and tries to make a u-turn, only to be cajoled by the elderly brain to stop in for some tea before embarking. Before the unsuspecting oxygen molecules know that something is afoot, they have already been inescapably ensnared in the never-ending account of the brain's mundane existence: how much they dislike the new labels on the cans of waxed beans, their unhappiness at the angle at which the Hendricksons park their bus, their ongoing see-saw battle with constipation, and on and on. There is no escape from such conversations. Rather than subjecting itself further to this anecdotal torture, the oxygen inevitably chooses to erase itself from being.

Making the geriatrics do jumping jacks speeds up the process two- or threefold.

Step two is installing a disco ball—a big one. Disco sheen is like cologne; you can never have too much.

Step three is the most important: Van Morrison's *Moondance*—the entire album, not just the song. Whatever you do, do not forget the *Moondance*.

But even with these remedies in place, it can still take years for your church to stop feeling like the inside of a second hand coffin. Furthermore, there is no guarantee that the atmosphere will ever return to normal. All you can do is keep "Caravan" on repeat and pray—and a fat lot of good praying will do seeing as you just transformed a house of worship into a bowling alley or an indoor laser tag center, or God forbid (really, He does forbid) a bar.

• • •

It had taken Stan nearly six months to get the oxygen in his church up to snuff, at least to the point where the customers didn't choke to death on their own boredom. Even so, the place still wasn't turning a profit. He just couldn't get enough people off the street and into the pews.

"I just don't get it, Lulu," he lamented to his little sister. "What do I have to do to get some people in here?"

Honolulu Adam was dusting the disco ball. Physically, she was the feminine version of her older brother, only far less undead-looking and smelling of lilacs rather than yeasty failure. Where Stan had a sallow complexion and morose countenance, his sister was a parcel of positive glow. She radiated warmth like good cognac which, like any recreational libation, she never touched. At the hospital where she worked as a nurse, most patients would have considered her a saint had they had any idea of what one was. They didn't, so they just thought of her as the fatty bit on the pork chop of life—the best part.

"Well, it might help if you had some beer," she surmised.

"There is *plenty* of beer!"

"That anyone would drink, I mean." The words wounded Stan. "I know you are trying and you're making progress," she sugar-coated. "Look at the last batch. It wasn't even poisonous. But let's be honest. *You* wouldn't even touch your beer with a ten-foot gondolier."

"I suppose you're right." She was right. Stan's inability to brew any potable beer, lager, ale, or stout had been a source of great frustration for him over the last few months. It wasn't really his fault, though. No one brewed beer on the Moon. Beer is sensitive to temperature and humidity and all that good stuff, but it is especially sensitive to gravity. There just wasn't enough of it on the Moon to make it work, at least through traditional processes. Stan was convinced, though, that with a few tweaks he could end-around the problem. So far he had figured out how to make Gouda cheese from barley, re-invented shoe polish, and given the glassware athlete's foot, but had not come remotely close to making anything resembling a beer-like beverage.

"But that still doesn't explain why I can't get people in here in the first place to at least *try* the beer. It's non-Euclidean geometry just to get anyone to set foot in here." Stan was beside himself in bewilderment. He had removed the dead birds and tilted the church upright. He had even added a new coat of elephant and installed a jukebox chock-full of Irish drinking songs, Journey, and *Moondance*. The location received ample foot traffic; the delicatessen and the empty lot were raking in the business. But try as he might, no one would give his little watering hole a try.

"You might think about changing the name," suggested Lulu.

"What's wrong with the name?"

"Well, it might rub people the wrong way. It just sounds so foreign and weird. Why couldn't you just use a normal name?"

The name of the bar was *Stan's*.

"But it's my name!"

"Your name is Stan*ford.* That's a name people have never heard before. It feels safe to them. Stan is too much like the old names, and no one trusts the old names. It just sounds a little pretentious and threatening. I know you're a history buff and everything, but maybe—"

"Yeah, yeah, I know," acquiesced Stan. He had learned all about it in one of his history classes. Stan had found the evolution of names to be a fascinating subject. He had gotten a B on the test.

• • •

Good-ole corn-fed American names had gone the way of the Diplodocus. They hadn't been snuffed out by a meteor, but rather had just worn out their welcome. History was filled with so many Alexanders and Michaels and Elizabeths who had accomplished such an endless array of feats that to give a child one of these names was perceived as being just as boring and unimaginative as ordering the same thing as the guy sitting next to you at the restaurant— or even worse, in some circles. To boot, naming your boy Alexander just set the bar way too high. Short of conquering Asia Minor or inventing the telephone, your son was doomed to live his life in the shadow of far greater men. So people everywhere took to the task of ensuring perceived success, or at the very least the absence of comparative failure, for all future generations. People needed to be individuals. You can't have other people going around invoking their name in place of yours. How could you expect to get ahead in the worlds?

"Did you hear about Cupboards Johnson?"

"The guy who owns that pizza place on the south side?"

"No. The other one."

"There are *two* Cupboards Johnson? That's unfortunate."

"A damned shame."

On the advice of daytime talk show hosts and televangelists, and other people who really matter, it was decreed that no two people should have the same name ever again. This policy ushered in a whole bundle of new, grandiose, and—everyone agreed—far better names. Gone were Tom, Dick, and Harry. In were Meatballs, Brick, and Crunchy. Now you could never be outshone by your predecessors. You simply didn't have any.

Round about the time Quesadilla the Primero was beginning his reign as King of Texifornia, names began to take on a whole different flavor. It was then that Dr. Rash MacDougal (almost) made the greatest scientific breakthrough of his career. In truth it was really the only scientific (almost) breakthrough of his career, as the rest of it had been wasted trying to prove that "everything is not as it seems."* Although that premise, which presented itself to Rash's brain in the form of a toga-wearing sea lion during a

---

* Dr. MacDougal is said to have developed the theory while hitchhiking around the galaxy with a band of busking bluegrass beatniks.

particularly ambitious foray into the land of booze and psychotropic drugs, had on the surface seemed like such a promising postulation, it never really lived up to the hype and was ultimately proven to be "not as good as I thought it would be." Rash would come to the same conclusion, reached interestingly enough through a similar combination of mind-altering intoxicants, about his attempt to give homosexuality a whirl. To each his own. Some people don't like pumpkin pie; so sue them.

Discredited by the scientific community and armed only with the knowledge that he really was an "only women— really" type of guy, Dr. Rash MacDougal recoiled into the shadows of society to live out the rest of his life in what he believed would be obscurity. But fate, which had been waiting impatiently in the wings for him to destroy his career as an intellectual, decided to change his life forever by injecting the soon-to-be Mrs. Rash MacDougal directly into the aorta of his existence.

It was lust at first sight; and after a less-than-lengthy seventeen-minute courting period, the two love birds set off down the hedonistic path that would lead them to their lives' calling: human reproduction on a mass scale.

Rash MacDougal may not have had much of a knack for scientific inquiry—outside of taking drugs—but he sure as hell had the cajones for it. Rash, it turns out, was the most fertile human male in the known universe. His genitals would become the subject of legends; and his wife, ever the eager participant, loved verifying these legends, over and over and over and over again. For her part, Mother Nature had surreptitiously bestowed upon Mrs. MacDougal an uncanny ability to rear children at a blinding pace. She is said to be the most efficient birther of children there ever was, able to furnish babes with extraordinary ease, exerting the same effort with which you or I might pass gas or daydream. Together these two sexual titans sired a family the likes of which had not been seen since Catholicism was in.

So precisely nine months and seventeen minutes after they had first laid eyes upon each other, Mr. and Mrs. Rash MacDougal, bucking the naming trend of the day, welcomed with loving affection the newest member of the MacDougal clan: Grace. Had Grace MacDougal been a bumbling, stumbling, stammering, dim-witted obstruction of a human being, there is no telling how the history of naming might have been different. But she wasn't. In fact, Grace MacDougal was the most fluid, articulate, balletic child anyone had ever seen. She nimbly danced through infancy with willowy elegance. Her twos were not terrible; never once did her virgin knees or elbows bear the unsightly blemishes borne by her awkward playmates. Her posture, always exquisite; her movements, lithe; her demeanor, ever calm. There was no denying it: Grace MacDougal had grace.

Being a man steeped in the scientific method, Dr. Mac-Dougal could not deny the obvious implication staring him directly in the face in the form of his seventeen-month-old, youngest member of the Russian Ballet of a daughter. He had named her Grace and she had grace. But the sample size was too small. He needed to run his experiment many times before his findings would merit any merit.

Without wasting a single minute, Dr. Rash MacDougal began plowing his wife with uninhibited vigor, setting into motion a process that would produce twenty-three offspring of varying size, gender, appearance, and ability; but who were all linked by a single, immutable, connective membrane: Their monikers meshed in perfect harmony with every quantum string fiber of their beings. (That's just a figure of speech, of course. Everyone knows that quantum string fibers don't mesh with anything. They exist in a state of chaos. And they make the worst sweaters.)

It began with Grace's first brother, Touchdown. He would go on to set single-game, season, and career records for every offensive category under the sun at Cutlery A. Smith High School, would be named All-Big Ten Athlete of the Century—twice—and never once in his nineteen year tenure as full-, half-, quarter-, and double-back for the Green Bay Packers would he lose a single game.

Emboldened by these early successes, Dr. MacDougal plowed on, each time bestowing upon his progeny the namesake that would be their calling. There was Class, who would have class; and Moneybags, who would eventually own sixty-five percent of everything. Phallus would become the 187th President of the United States, Moons, and Worlds of America; and Dick would become the producer of the most popular show on TV in which he, Dick, would point out to a television audience of 78 billion people the glaring deficiencies in the shape of each contestant's face. You may remember the show by its iconic tag line: *You might have at least one friend if your face didn't look like troll's vagina.* It was a big hit.

After posting his findings, parents from every walk of life jumped on board "Project MacDougal" faster than you can say "trend-o-ramma-jamma-doo." And for a good while the annals of what is now history were filled with the likes of Success the Great, Big Hands Baker, and Great the Great. But that all faded when, in a stroke of fantastic celestial irony, nothing was what it seemed, and it turned out that naming your child Nobel Prize in no way, shape, or form had any bearing whatsoever on whether or not he or she would receive one. The more ridiculous names were gradually phased out, and folks everywhere went back to feeling just fine about naming their child Latex or Hangover, or even Cupboards, without fear of being chastised. In the end, no one would remember Dr. Rash MacDougal for anything except for his balls.

In the summer of 2386 old, extinct institutions of higher education were all the rage—at least for names. There had been a time, believe it or not, when hordes of young people had paid top dollar to be herded into lecture halls and forced to listen to endless dissertations on this subject and that. These primitive scholars actually attempted, through a ridiculously cumbersome form of audio osmosis, to pluck knowledge right out of the air—as if it were a Frisbee or a soft fly to left-center—all in the feckless hope that at least some small percentage of the information could be retained. It hardly ever worked, of course; and once people had perfected the current practice of just baking Knowledge into meat pies and ingesting it directly, all those institutions fell into ruin. But the names lived on.

The lucky ones got in on the ground floor and snatched up such robust and promising names as Harvard, Duke, Baylor, and the like, whose recipients were granted immediate non-loser status in elementary school cafeterias and vestibules everywhere. But as it is with any trend, fashion or otherwise, there are those who just can't tell when it is time to get off the pot. These are the same people who insist on trying to bring back acid-wash denim wrestling singlets while simultaneously looking you straight in the eye through their leopard-skin monocle as they attempt to sell you vaudeville tickets. Or who name their child William-and-Mary. Worse yet, Brown. Naming your kid something that ridiculous should be a felony when slam dunks like Villanova and Michigan State are still on the table.

And so it was when Stanford A. Adam the First And Only was brought into this world—late and disoriented, as was to be his calling card for the rest of his life.

• • •

"I suppose I could give a new name a chance. What have I got to lose?"

Stan took down the placard above the door and gave it a remake. It took him a week to get it right. On the seventh day, he reinstalled it in its rightful place. He took a step back and admired his work. *This is good,* he thought.

The sign said: *Stanford's.*

Within ten minutes time, the place was brimming with drunk patrons belting out "Lovin' Touchin' Squeezin'" and taking the song to its literal conclusion with the bar maidens they had met only nine minutes earlier. Drinks were flying off the shelf.

Nobody dared touch the beer.

VI

What's in a Sandwich?

"So where does this guy say he is from again?"

"He says he's from some place called Earth."

"Earth? Never heard of it."

"No one has, sir. It's not on any of our charts."

"And he actually flew here? In that . . . craft over there?"

"Yes, sir. It appears so. I had the engineers take a look at it. They say it is propelled by a WFTL drive."

"Way faster than light?! No way!"

"I know it's hard to believe, sir, but it looks like we're dealing with a first-contact situation here."

"Well, that's just great. There goes my entire weekend. I suppose we'll have to put on a parade and everything."

"Ticker tape, sir?"

"Yeah, better give it all the bells and whistles. You know the drill."

"Yes, sir. Oh . . . and there is one more thing. He keeps going on about this sandwich. We can't make heads or tails out of it."

• • •

TO UNDERSTAND the Earthling fascination with bars, it may help to try to put yourself in their shoes. Having to live, as they did back then, must have been very taxing on their sense of self-worth. Remember that Earthlings at this particular moment in time were living smack dab in the custard-filled part of the Light Ages—the trough of Earthling self-confidence. The Light Ages had begun with the attainment of what Earthlings perceived to be a goal of fantastic merit, one that eclipsed the wheel and Dixieland jazz put together. They had finally, after painstaking years of failure, realized the capability to travel at the speed of light with less than a fifty-percent chance of perishing. Earthlings everywhere swaggered with jubilant vanity. Now that they could travel faster than greased lightning, they would really be able to go places.

And go places they did, at the speed of light and eventually even faster. Everywhere they went they planted their flag and built a YMCA. They had planned on teaching their new alien buddies how to play volleyball. It was the perfect sport for inter-species ice-breaking: You could play it with lots of beings in a small area, it didn't require any running, and you could even play it in the winter. Or on the beach. There wasn't a soul on the ever-expanding frontier who didn't dream of being the first volleyball ambassador to the would-be alien first contacts. The one problem with these would-be aliens, though, was that they just weren't.

Year after year, YMCA after YMCA, Earthling ambition gradually wilted like oven-baked dandelions. Despite having been zipping around at speeds exceeding the speed of light and despite having visited just about every moon, planet, and meteor in twenty-seven systems, the Earthling Empire had precisely bupkis to show for it. The known Universe had turned out to be nothing but barren wastelands and early suicides for investors banking on the hope that some new venture would produce, at the very least, a useful metal or valuable compound. Or a friend.

Man was sure he was alone in the Universe, and this drove him to drink. It didn't take long before all the YMCAs began selling beer on tap on all their racquetball courts and started using their volleyballs to vat whiskey.

The thing that had not occurred to these dimwitted little Earthlings was that although darting about at speeds in excess of 500,000 miles per second is not too shabby if you want to get to the next planet over, for the purpose of trying to explore the incomprehensible vastness of space it is akin to attempting to circumnavigate an aircraft carrier around the globe using nothing but a defective whoopee cushion for propulsion—only infinitely more futile. You would be better off trying to hold your breath and whistle "Yankee Doodle Dandy" at the same time. Moving at *any* speed isn't going to get you anywhere. The Universe is just way too prodigious.

It wasn't until Earthlings entered the Second Dark Ages that they finally got to empty the whiskey out of their volleyballs and start feeling good about themselves again. It was then that they discovered that traveling at the speed of light had been a frivolous hare-brained endeavor. Moving at the speed of *darkness* is where all the action is.

Light is to darkness what the tortoise is to UPS. I'll admit the whole arrangement is a bit unfair for light—and nobody tries harder, bless it—but when it comes to a foot-race, there really is no contest. Light never ceases trying to get where it is going as fast as it can get there, always a step behind its fleet-footed cousin, darkness. Rather, a more correct way of putting it would be to say that light is actually an *infinite* number of steps behind. Everywhere light travels, darkness is already there, waiting. Darkness is the roadrunner. It can never be bested.

Darkness doesn't have to *travel* anywhere. It's just there. The upside to this being that traveling at the speed of darkness—and here I use the word "speed" symbolically as speed has really nothing to do with it—gets you anywhere you want to be in no time flat. Upon hitching your wagon to darkness you are everywhere all at once. You don't even need a fancy-shmancy spacecraft to travel at the speed of darkness. All that is required is an open mind and comfortable footwear.

Lucky for Stan, the Light Ages were in full swing and Earthlings everywhere couldn't get to their bar stools fast enough.

"Who died?" mused Karl.

"Don't look at me," answered Stan. "Haven't checked the paper yet. But the funeral bus-pool lane was packed out on Aldrin. You know how it is this time of year, with the Mardi Gras celebration down in the French Quarter. It's a heart-attack convention down there." Stan had not gotten the joke.

"They would be better off handing out Big Macs instead of those beads," added Cramp Holden, the jovial delicatessen owner, as he slid onto his usual stool next to Karl at the end of the bar. "Was down there on Friday. They were expiring like yogurt coupons." Cramp, like every other business owner up and down 7th street, shuttered his windows by five p.m. With just about every customer preparing to climb into his single, separate bed, there was no reason to be open for business—unless you owned a bar and catered to the under-75s. Cramp was daily the first customer in the bar, barring Karl, who never actually left.

"Hey, Cramp. Good to see you. How about a beer to start you off?"

"Oooooh no," rejected Cramp, recusing himself outright. "I tested the last batch. Remember, I couldn't hear out of my right ear for three days, and every time I got hungry my vision went all wobbly. Get someone else to be your guinea pig. Just give me the usual."

"No need to get defensive about it. Just askin'. It *is* free, you know. I think we got a winner this time, Cramp. I really do." Stan clonked down a whiskey with a rye chaser.

"I was talking about your outfit, Stan, not that damnable parade," griped Karl. His phobia of choreographed marching performance arts was manifesting itself. He had played the tuba in his junior-high school band. First chair. The experience had scarred him for life. "What's with the black pajamas?"

"Oh, this? I was doing a little research. This little ensemble here is what priests used to wear. Figured if this place is a church then I should look the part." Stan was garbed in Johnny Cash from the toes up, except for a white collar. He even sported a rosary crudely constructed of a Mardi Gras necklace and a makeshift cross of tongue depressors and hot glue.

As the clock struck five, the usual crowd began their stampede into *Stanford's*. In the few months that had passed since Lulu made him change the sign, the place had really taken on an atmosphere befitting a proper hole-in-the-wall cesspool of debauchery. What little light that wasn't prismed off the disco ball oscillated from a spindly lattice of frayed extension cords and Christmas lights crawling along the inside walls of the nave like holly-jolly ivy. The lights, being the only thing with any distant relation to Christian culture that had survived the Chadic Conversion, were the only thing that lent the building any of its tenuous structural integrity. The ceiling, supported solely by the lights, was composed of an acrid blue cumulonimbus cancer jubilee that served to mask the natural olfactory ambiance of used *Hustler* magazines and downtrodden musk that otherwise lingered offensively in the air. Cigarettes, out of fashion for several-hundred years due to their carcinogenic tendencies, were *en vogue* once again after popular celebrities rediscovered their coolness and began smoking them in all the movies and sitcoms. As the patrons trendily puffed away their vitality, the ceiling gradually encroached on their headroom, making them paranoid and suspicious. This, more than the complimentary desiccated salt cubes, kept the customers buying drinks at a reckless pace.

A small chapel off to the side had been outfitted with a urinal trough, partitioned by a shower curtain to make a suitable place for the ladies—in the event that one should ever stay long enough to require the use of a lavatory. Above the bar, a single grainy screen displayed whatever Karl wanted to watch, being as he was the only person allowed access to the remote. Most of the time this was college football or reruns of *Dallas*, but today Karl had decided for everyone that the nightly boobery that transgressed on the idiot box was turning the men of *Stanford's* into witless dodos. He prescribed public broadcasting as the antidote. Luckily for them, he intimated, today just happened to be day three of a week-long live reading of every poem ever published by Emily Dickinson.

"Karl," warned Stan in a hushed tone, "you might want to lose the poetry. I don't think it's going over well with the customers."

"What makes you say that? Who doesn't like a little Emi D? I mean, just listen to this stuff."

Karl had failed to take into account the date. Tonight was the night of the big fight, the one that had been hyped for weeks, and more customers than usual had shown up to watch it at the bar. Sporting events are always better when drunk. Some, like bowling, lose meaning altogether without the anti-sobering liquid. They had come to *Stanford's* expecting blood and carnage to satisfy their morbid desires, but this—the Dickinson—was way too heavy. Insults were now being lobbed like Molotov cocktails.

"What the hell is this, Karl?! The fight's already started!"

"You've got exactly two seconds before I come over there and break your skinny little legs!"

"She doesn't strike me as a person who would wear white! Does she seem like that kind of person to you guys?"

Karl did not waver in the face of the choleric heckling. "Excuse me for trying to class up this joint." He was ready to take one on the chin for recluses everywhere before Stan snatched the remote from his pudgy fingers.

"I can't have fights breaking out before seven, Karl. We're watching the fight and that's final." Stan clicked the channel over to a swell of boisterous commendation.

The action had already gotten underway, and both fighters already showed signs of having taken a few licks in the previous round. The man on the right was bleeding from a gash below his left eye. Pretty soon he would lose all vision on that side as his face puffed up like country-club sensibility. His challenger didn't look quite as weathered, but it was clear that the people at *Stanford's* had already missed a good bit of clobbering. The bell rang and the two gladiators cautiously approached the podiums in the center of the squared circle. Every bar patron looked on in great anticipation as the second round of the Moon-wide gubernatorial election debate began. With pyrotechnics.

Elections were the number-one spectator sport on the Moon. Moononians, being on average old enough to go to the bathroom wherever and whenever they wanted, voted at the highest rate of any semi-autonomous democratic state in the Earthling known Universe—outside of Australia which thought it was a good idea to force every single illiterate schmuck to vote by edict of law. We all know how that turned out. Democracy shares a lot in common with Christmas carolers: A few people are enough to get the point across. After that, it just makes you want to pop someone in the nose. Besides, once *everyone* starts voting, what you've got is socialism, and we can't have that.

Puffy-eye opened on the offensive. *"Vote for this twit and I guarantee you that within a week of taking office, our beloved Moon will have been re-annexed by Florida and we'll all be speaking Russian with a lisp!"* The crowd roared as he landed the quip.

"Another baseless attack from my most unesteemed colleague. But don't let him fool you, ladies and gentlemen. Even as we speak, his moral turpitude is causing our orbit to decay. We don't have more than a week and a half before we are all drinking Mai Tais underwater in the Pacific Basin!" He had a point there. Without an orbit the economy would surely tank.

"This madman will increase the tax on analgesic creams by 7,000 percent!"

"This lunatic will turn you all into hermaphrodites in order to institute a repressive regime of uninhibited Caligu-monium!"

It was your typical political banter. None of it mattered anyway. The old folks would invariably vote for Silvertongue Sullivan,* just as they had in every election for the previous ninety-two years—despite the well-documented fact that Silvertongue had been deceased for the previous sixteen. People just went with what they were comfortable with. It wasn't like electing a dead person to political office was without precedent. Or merit.†

Stan didn't bother himself with the fight. He had learned a long time ago that mixing politics with his sauced nature was a recipe for Black Eyed Face. He instead focused his efforts on keeping the customers sufficiently watered without indulging himself. Lulu was going to be stopping by any minute, and if she noticed he was sampling the wares she would give him a lashing. She was all mint chocolate chip with everyone else, but with her brother Lulu dished it

---

*   Silvertongue was named during the MacDougal craze by parents who had wished him to be a snake-oil merchant, only to have their son double down and become a politician.

†   In the 2000 election the good citizens of the US state of Missouri knowingly voted in a deceased candidate rather than concede one of their two precious senate seats to the ass clown incumbent they had been saddled with for the preceding six years. On the order of Benny Hill, Lost To The Dead Guy was then promoted to Attorney General of the entire land. Hear, hear.

out straight as honky-tonk at a square dance. Stan was well aware that without her stabilizing presence in his life he would have long ago sold his lungs for a bottle of schnapps and was, in turn, grateful to his sister. Still, the urge to take the edge off a bit was awfully tempting. He focused on his work.

He scanned the room for empty glasses but stopped halfway like a public employee. In the front doorway was something remarkable. Just inside the heavy wooden threshold below the inviting sign that read *Stanford's* stood a pearl bust of feminine beauty. She was blonde and shimmering white light. Even those most engrossed by the realpolitik on TV were drawn to her angelic glow like a moth to used clothing. After thoroughly taking in her surroundings and covering her nose, she spied an empty stool at the end of the bar. It was the only place in the church where you couldn't see the TV.

The vixen pulled her body onto the bar stoop, rummaged through her handbag, and fished out a foreign device, one which had never been seen by anyone present at *Stanford's*. The woman took this mysterious contraption— which appeared to be constructed of many thin hand-sized opaque white membranes with horizontal lines decorating both sides, stacked one upon the other—and anchored it sturdily in her right hand. In her left hand she held an equally baffling implement, some type of slender wooden rod with a pointed end. It was all very peculiar. This woman was definitely not from around here.

"You're not from around here, are you?" said Stan as he ambled down to her end of the bar. Being a bartender, small talk was one of his strong suits.

"Just got in. How could you tell, Father?" As she said this she interfaced her rod with the membrane that happened to be on top, then squiggled the point methodically along the horizontal lines. A dry rustling sound escaped as if someone were polishing a chalkboard with a dead hamster. A filmy residue was left behind.

"Well, for one," said Stan matter-of-factly, eying the gizmo in the woman's hand, "there is that doohickey you're playing with there. Two, I've never seen you in here before, and I can't remember the last time a new sheep joined the flock."

"What? This?" She flailed her membranes in the air and looked at Stan like he was a pop-art sculpture. "It's a notepad."

"I see." He didn't see. "Then that would be . . .?" Stan elongated and raised the intonation on the "be." Earthlings use this speaking device as a clever way of signaling to an adjacent person to go ahead and finish the statement because the speaker hasn't the wherewithal to complete it himself. When the exchange is completed seamlessly, it's a great party trick. When it isn't, the sentence hangs out turgid in the air like male talent on the set of a dirty movie. This was one of those times.

"Er . . . so what would that be?" Here again, he received the incredulous look, but this time there was a hint of pity in the woman's eyes, as if Stan were a Cubs fan.

"This," she said, pausing for effect, "is a pencil." She probed deep into the recesses of his eyes for some spark of understanding. The flint had been replaced with an over-cooked fettuccine noodle. "I'm using it to write notes on this piece of paper here. See?" She turned the note-pad upside down and slid it across the bar so Stan could read it.

On it, written in loopy feminine letters, was:

> 27 parishioners
> hymnal jukebox
> sacred disco ball?

"I see." He didn't see. "Er . . . so what'll you be havin' today, Miss? Half price on all drinks and the beer is free. Well, the beer is always free. I can't give the stuff away."

"What's wrong with the beer?"

"Well, nothing is wrong with it, per se. I just haven't quite gotten the recipe hummin' just right yet. It doesn't always agree with the costumers. This is a new batch, though. I think we've got a winner this time. You could be the first to try it?"

"I think I'll just have the wine, Father. Just to be safe."

Stan reached back for a bottle of burgundy liquid, trying not to show the heartbroken look on his face.

"Half-price wine, Father? That's a new one. Is it some kind of charity event?"

"In a matter of speaking, yes," said Stan with a smile. "It's happy hour."

"Wait!" she shouted, stopping the words dead in their tracks as they were exiting his mouth. "Did you say . . . *hour*?" she whispered in a hushed cottony tone.

"Yeah. It's happy hour until six o'clock."

"Clocks?! Jesus, Mary, and Joseph!"

"Never heard of 'em. Who are they?" More scribbles on the membranes.

"You guys have clocks here?" she asked rhetorically. "Then that must mean that planet down there is . . . Earth!" Her eyes opened wide like distended beach-balls as something big and round dawned on her.

"Of course it's Earth, Miss. Are you feeling all right?"

"Oh, I'm fine. Fine indeed," she said with a noticeable hop-skip in her voice. Her whole demeanor had perked up.

"Sorry," she said meekly. "I do a lot of traveling. All these worlds look the same to me. You can't tell one from the other."

"I know what you mean," was Stan's reply, a statement which Stan himself believed to be the truth, but which most certainly was not. He did not know what she meant.

"Father, do you happen to have any . . . corned beef?

"Course we do. Best reuben sandwich this side of the Van Allen Belt. Would you like—"

"—Six! I'll take six! All with a double order of corned beef!"

"I'm sorry. Did you say you wanted *six* double corned beef reuben sandwiches?"

"Yes. Six reubens. *Double* corned beef," she repeated calmly and clearly as she began to regain her composure. She added an "if you would be so kind" to the end to make the Herculean order sound a bit more lady-like.

Stan blinked a couple of times, shrugged his shoulders, and smiled.

"Six reubens, double corned beef, coming right up."

• • •

What Stan didn't know was that ordering six double corned beef sandwiches was a dead giveaway. One might as well staple a billboard to his or her face saying: *I don't come from around here. I'm an alien. Now, take me to your leader, but only after you fix me that corned beef sandwich.* Aliens, whenever they visited Earth or any of its inconsequential colonies, would order, without fail, corned beef sandwiches by the truck-load. The reason being that the Earth systems were the only place in the Universe where you could get corned beef. That's just the way it was.

Some high up bureaucrat in the administration had thought up a little scheme to save a few bucks when the Universe was just getting off the ground. Worried about rising costs, he proposed that instead of filling the Universe with millions of different races, living on millions of different worlds in millions of different environments and costing kajillions of extra galacto-clams, they should just mass produce one single race and propagate it throughout the cosmos. The author of the bill suggested humans because he thought that monkeys were cute.

It was an idiotic idea and as such was passed into law lickity-split. Whole races of humans were rolled off the assembly line like Model-Ts. Each was placed on basically the same planet, and those planets were scattered throughout the Universe like bird seed on a matrimonial wind. The savings were tremendous. They were able to buy a new love seat for the 6th floor lobby with all the extra money.

The Universe was all set to be as boring as balancing your checkbook until an eleventh-hour addendum to the law provided for the smallest bit of diversity. One of the eggheads in the policy department pointed out that with all the life in the Universe acting as one enormous control, it would be the perfect time to run a few little experiments to see what really made stuff tick. It was decided that all the life-supporting planets in the Universe would be exactly the same, except for one thing. Every celestial body would be allotted one, and only one, extra spice. Just one thing that nobody else had.

So everywhere you went in the Universe, you saw humans. They were all the same race, lived on identical planets, breathed the same air, and had the same thing for breakfast—more or less. Sure, the languages and cultures developed a little differently, but that was really it. It was all the same. Except for that one thing that set it apart from all the others.

Some were bestowed with fantastic gifts. The humans of Fingolilly Four had cat-sized house pets called "gubs" whose gallbladders were filled with good luck. It tasted like foie gras. Everyone could perform a gallbladder-ectomy blindfolded by the time they were three, and as long as you made sure to play every bingo card, pachinko ball, and Pick-72 Power Lotto ticket you could get your hands on, you were destined to adore your existence living as a Fingolilly Fourian.

The people of the Vulovulu System were blessed with an internal organ which gave everyone bad breath whenever they told a lie. And this wasn't your average, garden variety, *haven't brushed in a few months* type of bad breath, either. We're talking real, home-cooked, nitrogen-curdling dragon breath. Deceit and deception were non-starters. Consequently, the Vulovs were the only society in the Universe to develop without politicians. It was a place where the inhabitants of Paradise went for vacation. That is, until mouthwash was discovered. Now the place looks like an exact replica of Gary, Indiana, and Aqaumint-O-Fresh flies off the shelf faster than toilet paper at the annual chili cook-off.

And then there were those who really got the crusty end of the burrito. The only thing the poor inhabitants of Gorko got was an extra shade of green. They had the most precise traffic lights in the Universe. Big whoop.

The planet that was shafted worse than any other, though, was Earth. The people of Earth were the victim of an unspeakable injustice. The one thing allotted to Earth was single-handedly responsible for what future scholars would come to call the Great Retardation of Earthling mental, physical, and spiritual growth. While the rest of the Universe had already grown weary of gallivanting all around creation in high-tech crafts and were instead focusing the bulk of their substantial powers on transferring their consciousness out of their lumbering, corporeal carcasses, the humans of Earth were still trying to figure out how to make their wheels roundish. Earthlings had gotten a bad shake. They had been given genitals.

Every other human race procreated by sneezing on each other. Earthlings, on the other hand, were required to couple through a gyrating mish-mash of bodily fluids. The problem with this secretionary mambo was that it felt a whole lot better than sneezing. Way better. Although it was a boon to the Earthling mattress industry, the downside was devastating. This shimmying, sluicing swap of genetic goop became the single solitary goal of every Earth male. It was the only thing that occupied his thoughts, and once realized the only inclination he had left, after taking a brief nap, was to figure out how to repeat the exploit at the earliest possible instant. Scientific inquiry and spiritual attainment were relegated to objectives higher in priority than universal healthcare coverage, but much lower than reality TV. The one hope Earth had for breaking out of its cognitive slump—the women—ultimately fell short. It wasn't their fault, though. They might have been able to get more work done were it not for the endless prodding and probing interruptions they received from their male counterparts. (This is not to say that the women didn't enjoy all the humping, pumping, smooching, smacking, slapping, slipping, dripping, gripping, gushing, flushing, mushing, moaning, groaning, boning, beeping, and discharging; because they did—by most accounts more so than the men. They were, however, able to function for more than four seconds without the need to perform, attempt, lay the groundwork for, fantasize about, or contemplate sexual gratification. Women could hold off on all that for at least enough time to squeeze in a sitcom.) After the magnitude of the blunder became evident, a special dispensation was granted and Earthlings were issued corned beef to make up for millennia of stagnation. Most still think Earth came out on top.

Earth humans were left to mature as stunted intellectual gremlins, trial-and-erroring their way though evolution like clueless light-bulb creators. It wasn't until first contact was finally made with the planet Farpthong in 8943 that Earth was hit by the reality of its position as low man on the totem-verse. The one-man vessel, piloted by the famous Capt. Felchin Furber, landed safely on the planet surface after three years, four months, eighteen days, thirteen hours, and nine minutes of zipping through the unbelievably boring nothingness of space, to great fanfare. There was a big parade. When told by his gracious hosts that he could have anything he wanted, on the house, for the duration of his stay, and after almost three and a half years of being nourished entirely by an IV drip and having only a few *Sports Illustrated Swimsuit Editions* for recreation, he immediately order a corned beef sandwich and a prostitute. All he received in return was a blank stare and a cold.

• • •

As she fervently munched away in gastronomic bliss, an odious desire was hijacking the thoughts of the mysterious traveler. She had been to just about every system they had a name for, but had never been to the little backwater they called Earth. But she *had* heard stories. And if this corned beef, this ridiculously delicious cured meat currently tumbling around her mouth, was any indication of what could be in store, things could get very interesting, indeed. Were she simply one of the rest of the sneezing humans that populated space, she would have been quite content to stop at the corned beef. But of course she was neither content nor human; she sold insurance. And her appetites extended beyond corned beef sandwiches.

"Father," she said in a low lusty tone, "do you mind if I ask you a personal question?"

"You know, you don't have to call me Father, Miss. I just wear this get-up to look the part. Truth is there hasn't been a real priest here since I won this church off the the last one in a game of five-card stud. Plain old Stan will do."

"Oh?" The woman's eyes widened.

"Stanford Adam at your service. And you can ask me anything you like."

"Okay, Stan. You are a male, right?" Stan liked the way the conversation had veered.

"Last time I checked."

"I'll take three shots of whatever is in that bottle there."

"The tequila?"

"That's the stuff. And pour a few for yourself while you're at it."

VII

Not in Nebraska Anymore, Toto

"There's no place like home. There's no place like home. There's no place like home. There's no place like—"

"Pumps, I told you. I already tried that. It doesn't work."

"Were your eyes closed?"

"Yes, my eyes were closed. The only thing that happened was my National Geographic getting stolen out from under my nose. Now I'm stuck with Newsweek."

"What's wrong with Newsweek?"

"It's all of six pages long. Do you know how much time I have to pass?"

"Well since you have so much extra time on your hands, why don't you try and locate me some ruby slippers."

• • •

THE MAGAZINE in Gumballs's hands was opened to the centerfold spread. The woman, posed beside a Bengal tiger, was wearing nothing but high heels and a power drill. She did not appear to be the bashful type. With her figure stretching out bodaciously before him like a nude accordion, Gumballs was positive she wasn't a man. One hundred percent.

"Ooooh, she's a doozy," piped in a feminine voice. Gumballs glanced left. Sitting in the chair next to him was a pair of oversized magnifying lenses tethered tenuously to the ears of a weathered brown syrup-bottle face.

"Yes, I was thinking something along those lines myself," said Gumballs.

"I could do without the drill, though. A bit over the top, don't you think?" She extended her hand. "Edith Tuttle, but you can call me Edie. Nice to meet you."

"It's a pleasure to meet you, Edie. My friends call me Gumby." Gumballs thought the drill was a nice touch. He was going to make a counterargument before his bearings took a reading and pulled over.

"I'm sorry, but where am I?" The last time he had this sensation was after spending the night with Stan, the bartender. He had ended up in Albuquerque—the one on Earth—as the keynote speaker for the annual convention of the National Association of Unlicensed Taxidermists. That was the last time he had had a drink or been allowed to attend a NAUT function.

"I could tell you were confused," consoled the old woman. "They always are when they first show up."

"First show up where?"

"Here." She rolled her eyes. "In the waiting room."

"Waiting room?"

"The waiting room. How else would you explain all this?" she said, waving her hand palm up, as if she were modeling merchandise on *The Price Is Right*. Gumballs extended his gaze past her fingertips and took in the rest of the scene. He and Edie were situated somewhere within a nondescript expanse that appeared to extend forever in all directions.

"How did I get to Nebraska?"

"They always say that, too, before they realize there isn't any corn."

There wasn't any corn—only cheaply upholstered chairs outfitted with human beings of every make and model for as far as his eyes could see. The chairs were divided into groups of about a dozen, each group besieging a black IKEA coffee table like the Ottoman Turks. The tables were haphazardly garnished with a mountain of overly fondled magazines. Kenny G was in the air.

"Do they always play Kenny G?"

"Oh, no," she reassured him. "Not *always*. Sometimes they throw in a little Michael McDonald."

Gumballs was reading, at the moment, a 39-year-old issue of *Unfettered Smut*. The soccer mom in the seat to his right was slathering him with contempt. Her teenage son was breathing heavily. Gumballs decided to add the magazine to the glossy sprawl on the table in front of him. He turned back to the old woman. "But what are we waiting *for*?"

"Waiting for our number to be called so we can be judged, of course. How else would you expect to make it into the afterlife? Have us all stampede through the front door at once? This isn't a soccer stadium, you know. We all have to be processed."

Gumballs could not help but wonder if he hadn't missed something rather important along the way. "Beg your pardon, Edie, but how did I get here?"

"I imagine you bit it."

"Bit what?"

"Kicked the bucket."

"You mean I . . ."

"Died. Yes, silly. There ain't no other way. What's the last thing you remember?"

"Well, let's see . . ." Gumballs racked his brain for a moment. "A woman materialized out of thin air, gave me a kiss on the cheek, and exited the bus—"

"The number 32?"

"Yes. Route 32. How did you know?"

"You guys have been popping up all over the place. I've already heard the whole story. There's an entire table over yonder with your friends around it. Must have been a pretty big accident."

"But I was just—"

"Best to put it out of your mind now. There is nothing to be done about it. You are not among the living anymore. Try one of the magazines."

This was not what Gumballs imagined being dead would be like. He had always figured it would be something like a stay at a luxury-hotel resort, where everyone was swaddled in fluffy white robes and received ayurvedic messages on the house; not a generic waiting room stocked with thirty-year-old magazines. "So how long have I been here?"

"Oh, you just got here."

"Well, how long have *you* been waiting?"

"Me? Oh, I've been waiting for a looooooooooong time. It isn't as if there is any incentive for them to move faster. Where could we go? No sir, they got us by the short and curlies."

The short and curlies were precisely what Gumballs hated being had by. Once they had you by those, the civility in the room evaporated to a level befitting an under-sober sporting event. He had to figure out a way to escape.

"And don't even *think* of trying to escape," she warned with a wag of her finger. "It can't be done. If they catch you they'll send you all the way to the end of the line."

"What if I have to go to the bathroom?"

"I wouldn't worry about that."

"But—"

"Just relax and read the magazines. Don't cause too much of a ruckus. You'll get us in trouble."

"But—"

"Shhhhhhhh!" Gumballs was silenced by his ten other tablemates in unison.

An authoritative voice resonated coldly from behind him. "Is there a problem over here?"

Gumballs turned to find a hefty woman with a clipboard and a stare that could freeze hydrogen. Her orthopedic shoes matched her white polyester pants.

"No no, Miss. No trouble here," covered Edie. "This gentleman here was just helping me find the most recent edition of *Gothic Housekeeping*. My eyes aren't what they used to be."

The polyester policewoman eyed Gumballs suspiciously. "I'll let it slide this time, but you know the rules. Any more from this table and I'll send you all back to the beginning. You'll be waiting *past* rapture after I'm through with you." The tone in her voice conveyed her conviction—cold and calculated as part-time deli help on the night shift.

After she had moved on, Edie really started giving him the business, careful not to look up from her magazine and incur any more wrath from the staff. "I told you. Best to keep your eyes on your magazine and your mouth shut."

She was about to drive the point home further but was interrupted by the loudspeaker. "Number twenty-seven. Number twenty-seven."

"Twenty-seven! That's me!" she exclaimed, the joy written on her face as obvious as a bad hair-piece. Around the table, everyone put down their magazines and applauded as she danced away into oblivion.

For the first time Gumballs could see everyone smiling. He joined in the genuine good feelings. Maybe this place wasn't so bad after all. He turned back to the soccer mom hoping to undue his first impression.

"So . . . do you wait here often?" he asked, stumbling right out of the gate.

Mummy Dearest didn't even give him the courtesy of a verbal response. She simply rolled her eyes skyward and shifted her position, flawlessly executing a *Can't you see I'm reading here?* economy-class, back-shoulder block.

Gumballs endured the attitude and plodded bravely into the one-sided conversation. "I know we got off on the wrong foot, but please understand that I was quite disoriented when I showed up. I don't even know how I came to be reading such an . . . unsavory monthly. I assure you I am not one to read such drivel in public. I meant no disrespect. I hope you and your boy a will accept my apology."

The soccer mom didn't so much as flinch.

"Well . . . so, twenty-seven, huh? I imagine we are moving right along, yeah? What number did you get—if you don't mind me asking?"

Without looking up from her magazine she reached into her pocket and brandished a slip of paper. She supplemented the gesture with an acrimonious snort:

64

"Sixty-four, huh? Well that's good news, now isn't it? That's right around the corner. I bet you'll be out of here in no time."

This time the woman flinched, but only to return the slip to her pocket.

"So . . . where does one get one of those slips anyway? I suppose I should probably grab one quick. I don't think I want to hang around here any longer than I have to."

Just then a deli counter number dispenser materialized like a summoned genie right in front of Gumballs.

"Well, isn't that convenient," he said as he plucked a number from the the dispenser's mouth. "Let's see if Lady Luck is on my side:"

$$\infty + 9$$

Apparently, the Lady had a bone to pick.

Gumballs tried to remember back to Mrs. Vandenhooten's math class. Subtracting 27 from $\infty + 9$ in his head, he came up with the difference: *This was going to take a while.* He gave and elongated sigh and picked up last month's issue of *Play-nine.* It opened to the centerfold spread—a cocker spaniel posed with a Bengal tiger.

A conspicuously audible *pft* interrupted his discouragement as he felt a presence coalesce in the open seat just vacated on his left.

"What is Beowulf!"

"Shhhhhh!"

VIII

THE GENERALS

"Ow! Are you sure you've done this before?"

"What gave you the impression I haven't?"

"Well, for starters I think that is designed to go in there, and those should probably be left off to the side for now."

"What about these?"

"Less twisting, I think."

"You'd think this doodad would come with a manual."

"Ow! I said LESS twisting!"

• • •

*S*HALL *I fix you a drink?* would most certainly have been the proper prompt, given the situation. A savvier man would have conjured up some semantic alchemy laced with wit and innuendo, but Stan was not such a savvy man as that. Especially in his current state. Winston Churchill or

Mark Twain could have done it, no problem—produced some keen line tying together hard liquor, the wonder bra, and the power of suggestion into one provocative little parcel bursting with smooth and itching to be unwrapped like Christmas-morning rug-rat fodder. But those men— dynamos of rhetoric—were confined to the annals of history, only to be heard from by those fortunate enough to have television dials capable of reaching channel 252[8].

So *Shall I fix you a drink?* was what Stan said—or at least intended to say. Carefully crafted and engineered in a factory of ill-firing synapses, the suggestion initially rolled off the assembly line in tip-top condition—all shiny and new, complete with the smell of untainted synthetic leather. But somewhere en route, most likely in the sinuses or around the medulla oblongata, the whole thing fell to pieces like a set of Soviet lawn furniture. What was once the Rolls Royce of ice-breakers reached its destination, that being Stan's mouth, as only a belch-like facial convulsion. Too many consonants for a man in such an inebriated state. His old nemesis—alcohol—had reared its room-slanting head once again. The vile poison had slowly, yet not unpleasantly, stripped Stan of all his prowess, ability, and motor function. It was a familiar pattern which Stan had seen crop up repeatedly during his thirty-plus years of professionally studying the bottom of liquor bottles, though he wasn't alone in his practice of the intoxicated method.

• • •

A peculiar thing, alcohol. Most peculiar of its attributes is the continued peculiarity it has managed to maintain, eon after eon, in the eyes of the whole of the human race. To mankind alcohol is as baffling a substance as has ever been discovered, more so than vegetarian chili or even parachute pants. Through painstaking stick-to-itivness, Man had somehow managed to blunder and grope his way from fire to the wheel—all the way up to Wrestlemania—yet he could not, for one single second, wrap his noodle around the conundrum that was alcohol. Try as he might—and, boy, did he ever try—Man just couldn't work out the three—and only three—things one needs to know when it comes to alcohol: One, it can provide short-term enjoyment. Two, it provides less enjoyment in the mid- to long-term. Three, when consumed in adequate amounts, all memory of the short-term enjoyment is stricken from the drinker's mental record, leaving the participant holding only a big sweaty bag of mid- to long-term compunction. An outside observer would think these facts to be elementary and self-evident, yet to Man this simple trilogy of knowledge was too dense to float to the top of his cocktail where he could have easily ascertained it. Instead he resigned himself to testing this mystery fluid over and over and over until he damn well got to the bottom of it—the mystery or the bottle.

Thus, alcohol consumption became the longest-running continuous experiment undertaken by humankind. For thousands of years alcohol had been painstakingly ingested so that its effects could be studied on everything from hand-eye coordination to bladder control. It's not clear what everyone expected to gain from such in-depth scrutiny and re-experimentation—a causal shortcoming not unrelated to the fact that the experimentation itself tended to lend its participants to straying from the rigid path of the scientific method and instead traipsing zigzaggedly down the oft-unbeaten deer trail of booty calls and skinny-dipping in capes—but the results were undeniable and well-documented.

Like fermented clockwork, the devilish liquid robbed its victims of their faculties in a predictable, yet unavoidable, precision order. The first stage still had a rather pleasant—in some cases, therapeutic—polish to it. Tongues were loosened to the point where making conversation with the person across from you did not feel punitive.* Tension in the shoulders and around the brain stem was eased, ever so slightly, facilitating the ogling, boggling, and wobbling states of being most natural to Homo sapiens. From there Man's aptitude for coherent existence exited stage left with greater gusto than a den of Cub Scouts at an all-you-can-eat Mongolian barbecue.

The next symptom to manifest itself was the inability to throw strikes,† and from there the inevitable decline contin-

---

* In most modern justice systems, the penalty for grand larceny is two hundred hours of small talk. In others they just chop off your hands. Scholars still consider it "pretty much a toss-up" as to which one is more cruel.

† See: *Entire Chicago Cubs Pitching Staff* circa 20th century.

ued, mercilessly: Pupils, handicapped, could no longer focus on anything other than the bulging regions of the human physique; the digestive system ceased functioning at optimal levels, able to process only pizza and deep-fried gyros; and the wires in the speech center of the brain got all crossed-up, resulting in prepositional phrases being substituted out in favor of vomit—which invariably tasted like pizza and/or deep-fried gyros . . . and vomit. If the subject continued on his (or her, but more often than not, his) hedonistic path, even the contents of his bowels would eventually abandon ship, ruining much more than just the evening.

• • •

It took Stan a moment to register the shortcoming of his elocution. He pressed on, determined not to let a silly little thing like his tongue get in the way of speaking his mind. The last time he had taken home a woman with the express purpose of receiving, voluntarily, an exchange of any form of sordid country business had been during the Cretaceous period. The Magna Carta, the printing press, and cherry cola had each since marked Man's successive advancement on the ladder of evolutionary headway. It was unfortunate that Stan had not been able to translate this knowledge into more tangible carnal capital.

"I'm a nice guy, right, Lulu?"

"You're an asshole."

"Well, yeah, but—"

"And you never met a drink you didn't like."

"Well, yeah, I have a drink every now and then. But I'm not a bad-looking guy, right?

"I'll give you that. You're not a gargoyle."

And he wasn't. Besides a slight hitch in his gait, a barely noticeable glare in his gaze, and a bit of excess girth in several places where it was not typically deemed to be appealing—but mind you, a sufficient amount in all the places where it was*—Stan was not too offensive to look it. He bore no unsightly marks above the shoulders. His smile was on the right way. And his penchant for neglecting to shave gave him a peaty type of rustic feel that looked good on him, but could, on occasion, leave others looking like used-tire salesmen or out-of-work Neanderthals.

He came about for a another volley. "Canafex rink?"

"Honey, I don't think you need another drink. I think you need to open a window. Do you have a dog?"

Stan did not have a dog. He did, however, have a collection of biodegradable refuse which led one's nose to believe they were in the presence of a decomposing terrier. Taking stock of his apartment, even Stan himself was taken aback. He couldn't remember the last time he had been sober enough to recall being home, but he was almost positive this was the place. The scene before him looked like a horror-film movie set constructed entirely out of cream cheese and left out in the sun over the summer. Where the sofa had

---

*   Stan, I must say, *did* have one divinely defined set of calves on him.

once been there was now only a love seat-shaped compost heap. The floor had grown sentient and was now exhaling and inhaling in pulsating, wavy breaths, making it increasingly difficult to walk. In the corner, he was surprised and delighted to find a garden of microwavable burritos. He told himself to remember to water them when he had the chance. He fully expected his date to toss back up the reubens and tequila right then and there, and was somewhat disappointed when she didn't. It would have helped with the smell.

Never before had Stan encountered such a woman. The only thing he knew about her was that she was a traveling insurance agent who had never been to the Moon, or Earth, and that she seemed to feed her libido with corned beef. On top of that, she drank like an Irish Booze Hound. Even Stan, permanent resident and de facto mayor of Hootchville, had found it difficult to keep up.

Tall, blonde, fit, buxom—the woman who had followed him back to his apartment was the most stunning creature he had ever laid eyes upon. Even before the dozen warm-up shots of tequila, he had found himself salivating over her angelic beauty. Most nights Stan would count himself lucky if he got a woman without an eye patch to notice him.* Now he was being actively courted by Helen of Troy. He

---

*   Stan was often quick to point out that this feat wasn't as easy to accomplish as everyone made it out to. He argued that getting a woman who had only half the noticing ability of the average female to notice you should entitle you to some extra credit, but Karl and the boys would have none of it.

marveled at her body as she cleared away enough refuse to find the compost heap, each bulldozing maneuver producing the kind of motion reserved for celestial bodies. A subsequent examination of the temptress revealed little that could be shown on public television—in The States, at least. In Europe, most everyone on TV is naked. It must be very embarrassing for them.

"Now, Father," she said playfully, "let's see what all the fuss is about." She fixed Stan in her cross-hairs, reared back like a rabid stallion, and charged double-quick, gnashing her teeth and giving the rebel yell. She creamed Stan like a unblocked linebacker on a naked bootleg. It was like something out of a late-night Cinemax special.

Before he knew what was going on, Stan found himself in the camel clutch. Vim and vigor are never bad things when they apply to an extra-curricular rendezvous, but too much pep can spoil the bouillabaisse. He decided that any more foreplay would risk dislocation of something important and went instead straight for the meat and potatoes.

Using an ottoman and a drift of half-eaten Chinese food for leverage, he managed to free himself from the submission move. Sprightly dodging the ensuing leg drop, he pounced and fumbled around her back until he found the clip to his salvation. Most brassieres implemented a simple two-hook system. Although slightly foreign to the average male at first, this obstacle could easily be neutralized through a little practice and dedicated finger-dexterity exercises. Sadly, Stan had drunk away every last ounce of dexterity. Feeling his chance of taking this thing to the next level without having to endure major injury slipping away, he decided to take the only option left to him: the Drunk Man's Chomp and Chew. He hooked the first lace strap he could find with his mandibles and said a prayer. It was answered.

In a heavenly release, two magnificent voluptuary brigades, previously bivouacked behind protective white-satin encampments, spilled forth like the Mongol horde. Where once there was quiet all along the eastern front of his dormant loins, there was now a great deal of fidgeting and panic. In the trenches along the line, Stan's abstinential fortitude, confronted with the enemy's substantial feminine armaments, sent up the white flag expeditiously in an act of salivating, oggly-eyed surrender. General Lee and Napoleon, as Stan had taken to calling them, marshaled the attack. The rout was on.

What followed was a blur of elbows, headboards, and tantric locomotion; a scintillating cacophony of exploratory hoo haw and explicit sexual judo. There were more *oohs* and *ahs* than a Japanese cooking program, and twice the *harrumphing*. Toes curled. Backs bent. Guiness records shattered like dreams of pie-in-the-sky. Neighbors were brought to the brink of calling the police only to ditch their phones mid-dial in favor of video-recording equipment which—this tale taking place in your distant, super high-tech future— was actually *attached* to their phones, if you can believe that. Everyone just flipped their devices around and *voilá*.

When all the centripetal lust finally pittered out and an end came to the sumptuous, lewd rumpus, the two participants rolled to a stop in a spooning position.

"Holy Moley!" exclaimed Stan. He thought for a moment, then said the only thing that came to mind:

"Holy Moley!"

The fact that he was now divulging information of the most exhibitionist nature to every video-recording device in the neighborhood did not matter to him in the slightest. He had turned European. And he was in love. Now he only needed to find out what this woman's name was and he would really be in business. He opened his mouth to speak, but the words were ambushed in the back of his throat by the advancing declarative vanguard of his new lover. Stan's words turned and ran. They were yellow-belly words.

"Yeah, yeah, I know," she interrupted. "Holy Moley. Now, you don't happen to have another one of those reubens lying around here, do you?"

IX

LOVE AND WOOKIEES

"Lulu, I think my mirror is on the fritz. It's not producing any vanity."

"What's the problem?"

"My face."

· · ·

LULU HAD been pounding on the front door for five minutes before she managed to rouse Stan. He came to the door in a frightful state. For starters, there was a Wookiee squatting in his head. His new guest had taken the liberty of cramming the whole of his brain off to one side of his skull to make room for a den in which to hibernate through the weekend. The world, as it appeared through Stan's eyes, had taken on a yellow mustard hue, and the thought of breathing made him want to throw up. He dragged himself to the front hall unsure if the Wookiee's remodeling had caused a stroke while he was sleeping or if he had just forgotten the right side of his body in bed. The pounding on the door synchronized with the drumming behind his eyes.

"Lulu! For goodness sake, would you please stop that pounding," he complained as he unbolted the lock. Lulu burst threw the door, sending Stan flying back into the vestibule. If it hadn't been for the mossy growth on the floor, he probably would have cracked his head open and sent Chewie spilling into the front hallway.

"Where have you been, Stan!" She had not even bothered to notice the mass of older brother wasting away on the floor and instead jumped right into the tirade she had been practicing in her head ever since she discovered the bar open, unattended, and doling out free drinks like a democrat, after popping into *Stanford's* after her shift ended the night before.

"How could you do that, Stan?! Just when the bar was starting to at least break even. How could you just leave it, unattended for those drunks to drink you—us—dry?! How could you be so—" She finally turned around to face her brother. "For Pete's sake, Stan. Would it kill you to put some pants on?"

"Oh, settle down. You're a nurse. Not like it's nothing you haven't seen before."

"Oh my G—What the hell happened to your face?!"

"Would you stop your yelling! I can't take loud right now, not before I get some coffee in me."

He stumbled into the bathroom to cover himself in a robe and splash some water on his face. The face that greeted him in the mirror did not belong to him. It belonged to the person who put "The Animal" in between George Steel's names. It turns out the nickname had nothing at all to do with George's prowess in between the sheets. One of Stan's eyes was completely swollen shut; his nose now included a few extra right angles; and his upper lip was shaved—off. These injuries, in addition to a multitude of cuts, bruises, and second-degree burns, camouflaged his body with red, purple, and pus from head to toe.

"I told you not to talk politics. Why don't you sit down and let me fix you up." She guided him to the sofa-like structure in the front room and searched for materials hygienic enough to be used in first aid. "What happened? Does it hurt?"

Hurt did not even begin to describe what he was feeling at the moment. Hurt was the sensation you got when you tried to fix the lawn-mower without first turning it off. It was the result of substituting laundry soap for protein in your diet, or the grievous response your soul experienced while watching C-SPAN. What Stan was feeling at the moment was far worse than any of that. He was in love.

"I met someone, Lulu."

"Where? In a dark alley? Were you mugged?"

"She didn't mug me, Lulu. She made love to me."

"Who?"

"The woman—"

"What woman, Stan? There isn't anybody else here."

"Of course there is. She's right over—" He stopped as he came to an awful realization. "She's gone!"

"Who? Who is gone?"

"I . . . don't know. I never got her name."

"Are you drunk already?"

"Of course not." He was not drunk already; he was drunk *still*—the difference of which Stan was well acquainted. One couldn't go to work if he were drunk *already*, where it was perfectly acceptable, expected even, to do so when one was drunk *still*. The same rule did not, however, apply to job interviews. Stan had learned that one the hard way.

• • •

"Please come in and thank you for—Are you drunk already?"

"Of course not, sir. What kind of a person would come to a job interview drunk already?"

"Then how do you explain the fact that I'm getting drunk just sitting here talking to you?"

"That's not me talking, sir. It's the booze. Still hanging around after the bachelor party last night."

"On a Monday?"

"Monday, Wednesday, Saturday—I don't discriminate."

"So you are drunk *still?*"

"Right you are, sir. Did I get the job?"

• • •

"Stan, tell me what happened. I'm starting to worry."

"Lulu, I met the most amazing woman last night. She came into the bar and started buying me shots of tequila."

"That's your idea of the most amazing woman? One who buys shots of tequila for you?"

"Well, actually, it was—until last night. But she was so much more than the tequila, Lulu. You should have seen her—beautiful, radiant, intelligent—and no eye patch."

Lulu rolled her eyes.

"I was just going to have one, just to to be polite, you see. And then one thing led to another—"

"So you decided to leave the bar unattended so you could shack up with this floozie?!"

"No, I wouldn't do anything stupid like that. I left Karl in charge."

"That still doesn't explain why you look like you've been put through the garbage disposal."

"Oh that. Well, she's a bit—uh—how should I put it . . . aggressive."

"*She* did this to you?!"

"*We* did this to me, *together*. Love hurts, you know. Can't expect to crack open a bottle of passion without a concussion or two."

Lulu had heard quite enough. She was now scanning the room for a bat or a club—a nine iron, in a pinch.

"You're telling me that you decided to leave the bar—the bar that is in danger of being repossessed by the bank—in the hands of your drunk degenerate friend so you could take some stranger home to wrestle with?"

"It was *love* wrestling, Lulu."

"STAN!!" Stan had rarely seen his sister in such an aggravated state. She was fuming around the living room, kicking up refuse and unripened microwavable burritos. "How could you do this to me, Stan! *I* was the one who co-signed the loan on the church. *I* was the one who helped teach all those senior calisthenics classes. I *even* installed that damned disco ball! Disco has been extinct for—"

"Disco is *not* dead!" Lulu shot him the banshee-on-the-rag sneer. *Proceed with extreme caution.* "Listen, Lulu—"

"A man from the bank came to see me this morning, Stan. They are going to foreclose unless we pay up."

"You mean—"

"We are going to lose everything, Stan. EVERY-THING!" Her words hit Stan like a custard pie.

"But—"

"EVERYTHING! "

"But I'm in love."

"Face it, Stan. You were used. She test drove you, kicked your tires a bit—"

"That's not all she kicked."

"Damnit, Stan. Can't you see? You will never see her again. You don't even know her name!"

"Lulu, you're my sister and I love you. And more often than not—a great deal more often than not—you are right. But you have to trust me on this. This woman is the best thing that has ever happened to me."

Lulu was now doing her impression of Krakatoa.

"She left! She won't ever be back! And she sure as chicken pox won't help you out with your money problems!"

Before she could get any further, Stan spotted something on the coffee table. Apparently, the love of his life had not left him high and dry after all. She had left a note. It had been written in pencil on a small piece of notebook paper in loopy feminine letters. It read:

> 27 parishioners
> hymnal jukebox
> sacred disco ball???
>
> Stan,
> Popped out to pick up some supplies. Will be back soon.
>
> —Wanda
>
> P.S. I can help you out with your money problems.

• • •

Lulu had just finished clothing her brother and straightening his nose when she heard a rustling in the front hall.

"Stan? Are you awake, honey?" carried a voice through to the living room.

"We're back here."

Wanda entered the room carrying two shoe boxes, a grocery bag full of first-aid supplies, and potpourri—coconut musk. Lulu stood to size her up.

"Just who do you think you are?"

"Oh, you must be Lulu. I was hoping to meet you. We have much to talk about, you and I." She set down the boxes on the kitchen table and extended her hand. "My name is Wanda. It is a pleasure to meet you." Lulu took the hand reluctantly.

"Lu—"

"Lulu Adam. I know all about you."

"You do?"

"You're the one who put up the money to renovate the church, not to mention the one keeping it afloat while it's been operating at a loss all this time."

"How did you know that?"

"I don't have time to go into it in great detail right now, but suffice it to say that the people I work for have taken quite an interest in both of you—and the church, of course."

"An interest?"

"Long story short, we want to see the church succeed, and we would like to help you out."

"Is this your idea of helping out?" Lulu pointed to the lump of bandages wheezing away on the couch. "I'm pretty sure he has a punctured kidney, and there is no telling how long it will take to reattach all these retinas. Did you do this to him?"

"I'm afraid I did. I'm terribly sorry. I feel awful over all the bruising. I had never had—What were we drinking last night, Stan?"

"Tequila."

"Yes, that's right. I had never had tequila before, and it packed a bit more punch than expected. Got a little carried away. I hope you'll forgive me."

"Carried away? Look at him. He—"

"Would you two stop worrying," piped in Stan from the couch. "I'll be fine as soon as I get some coffee in me."

"Oh, you poor thing," cooed Wanda. "Just hold on a second. Help is on the way." She walked over to the table and returned with the shoe boxes, handing one to Lulu.

"I'm going to need you to put these on. There is no way you can travel in those stilettos." Lulu opened the box to find a pair of hand-stitched leather moccasins.

"What's wrong with these heels?"

"Oh, nothing at all, honey. I think they are adorable, but they won't do to travel in," said Wanda, fitting Stan with his own pair of moccasins.

"Where are we going?"

"I've got to get both of you to headquarters. Boss wants to see you right away."

"But I've got to work this afternoon."

"Lulu, my dear, this is not the time to be worried about a silly little thing like lifetime employment. We've got to get some help—stat."

"A hospital?"

"Financial help. We've got to save the church."

"What about Stan?"

"Stan—well—yes, him too. But time is of the essence. You're going to have to trust me on this one. Now please get those moccasins on and grab hold of my hand." Wanda took a deep breath and closed her eyes.

"Now hold on just a minute. I—" started Lulu, but before she could argue any further, an ultra-low frequency burping sound erupted from the globular hole that had opened in space-time in the place where the coffee table had been.

Wanda propped up Stan and stepped toward the void. "All will be explained to you soon, but right now we've got to move. Now would you please take my hand."

The only thing Lulu remembered after clasping Wanda's outstretched hand was darkness and the odd sensation of being everywhere all at once. It felt like having brunch with Timothy Leary.

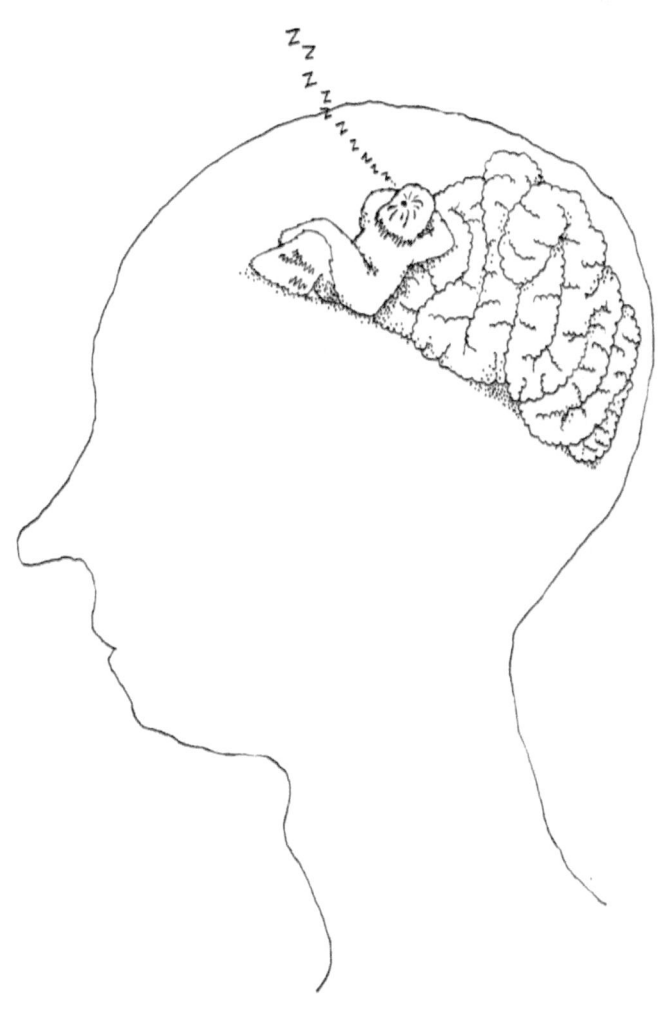

X

THE PUDDING

"So what do you guys eat around here, anyway? I could go for a little grub."

"Sorry, the missus has me on diet. The only thing I can offer you is a shot of wheat grass or ants-on-a-log."

"You didn't tell me you were married. Is she here?"

"Oh, yes. She's here. She's always here."

"Well that must be nice."

"Oh yeah, it's just fantastic having a wife who knows where you are at all times, knows every mistake you have or will ever make, and can hold a grudge until the end of forever. It's A-plus lemon fuck-dandy swell."

"How's her meatloaf?"

"Not bad, actually."

. . .

THE LAST time Stanford stepped into a heaping blob of pudding-like goo, he ended up coating his boots with the output end of a canine colonic equation. The result was less than aromatic. This time around, the same action yielded far different results.

Being "in the pudding," as he would later describe it to Karl, was unlike anything Stan had ever experienced. It was, in fact, nothing like anything that anyone from Earth had ever experienced. Stan, along with his younger sister, Lulu, had the distinguished honor of being the first Earthlings to go omnipresent—to move at the speed of darkness.

In its natural form, "darkness" is said to be the most unimaginably beautiful construct. The nothing, they say, is really something. This is all a matter of perception, mind you. Omni*presence* can only be "correctly" perceived when supplemented with additional proficiency in both omni*science* and omni*potence*. Together these three faculties make up the holy trinity of om-nazingness. What Stan experienced was a state of all-being, simultaneously and instantly saturating every single iota of the Universe like dung-fire smoke in a yurt. By himself, Stan wouldn't have had the slightest chance of achieving such a feat. But Stan happened to have a guide—he was holding Wanda's hand. Essentially, he was being dragged Everywhere, all at once. This entire process didn't actually take any time, either, since the moment he disembarked from his living-room on the Moon was also the exact same moment he arrived at his destination—presto-chango. Perception, though, was really giving him the business. His pitiful excuse for a perceiving organ—his paltry brain—was doing its darnedest to take in the whole all-being thing, but because Stan was neither all-knowing nor all-powerful, he *perceived* his first taste of ubiquity with about as much comprehension as a piece of rhubarb pie could correctly perceive *Dante's Inferno* transmitted in Morse code via seismic P-waves emanating from a polka-dotted stegosaurus's ass, in reverse: He didn't have a fucking clue what was really going on.

To be sure, there are plenty of omnipresent, omniscient, omnipotent beings billowing around "out there" who have no trouble at all taking in "darkness" in all its splendor and glory, and they enjoy nothing more than describing it in detail to anyone who can conceive of understanding such an ethereal vista—as long as they are all-knowing, -being, and -powerful. If you don't happen to cut their cliquey mustard, though, you had better brace yourself. They can act like a bunch of holier-than-thou, know-it-all pricks. Travelers beware.

In Stan's case, he found himself (at least he perceived) in the presence of one of (if we were splitting hairs we might say "all of," but again, it's a perception thing) these om-nazing beings while ensconced "in the pudding." This isn't at all surprising. Traveling at such a pervasive speed, you can scarcely go anywhere without running into one. They're Everywhere.

"Well, hello there, sir!" greeted Stan instinctively. As far as he could tell, he was in the middle of a heated game of backgammon with a gentleman in a top-hat and a handlebar mustache, who happened to be smoking a Chinook salmon. Stan, Mr. Top Hat, and the backgammon all seemed to be jogging in place atop a 1994 olive-drab Volkswagen Golf adrift on a sea of breakfast-cereal marshmallows.

"Oh, this is just great—a newbie." The palpable sarcasm in the man's voice was perceived by Stan as grapefruit pulp blobulating through the air encased in comic-book dialogue bubbles. One of these sarcasm globs collided with Stan's face and left a pink stain. It stung like the dickens— and those sting a lot. Grapefruit pulp in the eye is no picnic.

"I beg your pardon, sir, but I wonder if I might take up a moment of your time. Do you happen to know—"

"I know *everything* there is to know," gloated the man, puffing ostentatiously on his salmon.

"Wonderful! Then perhaps you wouldn't mind telling me where we are?"

"*Where?* How quaint. This one's right off the turnip truck, boys!" he pronounced into the air. "You honestly don't know, do you?"

"Well, no sir, I—"

"—Rhetorical. Of course I already *know* that *you* don't know. I'm an OBOE."

"An Oboe? Like from *Peter and the Wolf?*"

"O.B.O.E.—Omni-Being Of the Everywhere."

"Omni . . .?"

"—present, omniscient, omnipotent—Omni-Being. But you can just call me Kevin."

Stan was trying to take this all in. Being all-knowing would have come in pretty handy right then.

"Golly, Kevin, that . . . being all that omni-everything . . . must really be something."

"It's not all it's cracked up to be, believe me."

"Does that mean that I am, at this moment . . . *Everywhere?*"

"That's the first almost-intelligent thing you've said yet."

"So . . . why are there breakfast-cereal marshmallows . . . Everywhere?"

"There aren't."

"And why isn't Wanda or my sister here with me?"

"They are."

"Sorry, but am I missing something?" Stan's non-mniscient brain was overheating like an 8-bit motorbike.

"That's the second almost-intelligent thing you've said."

"Look, Kev," said Stan, not caring for the tone in the voice breezing past the salmon smoker's handlebar mustache. "I don't know what I've done to get on your bad side, but this a first for me. I'm a little out of my league here."

"That's the third almost—"

"—So, if you could just toss me a bone, I would really appreciate it."

"All right," acquiesced Kevin. "Since it is your first time . . ."

"Thank you."

"Long story short: Marshmallows do not constitute all matter in the Universe; Wanda and Lulu are here, as are you and I, and everyone, and everything. You are omnipresent, remember."

"Uh . . ."

"Now, your feeble little intellect can make neither heads nor tails of all this information, so it is, instead . . . electing to perceive things thus." He opened his arms wide like a magnanimous prophet, being careful to first secure the Chinook in his teeth so as not to drop it.

"I see," said Stan. He did not see. "So I'm *choosing* to perceive marshmallows as the building-blocks of life?"

"In so many words, yes."

"Why do you suppose I'm doing that?" Here Kevin just rolled his eyes back into his head and sighed dickishly.

"Never mind," backtracked Stan. He decided to steer the conversation onto a new vector. "So . . . what does an all-knowing, everywhere-being, all-powerful fellow, such as yourself, do for fun? It must be a gas."

"Nothing could be further from the truth. You try knowing everything that is, was, or ever will be and tell me how much fun *you* have. No surprises. No intrigue. No discovery. No excitement."

"I guess I never thought about it like that."

"No thinking, either. Who needs to think when you already know?"

"Well, you must have a hobby or something? What do you do in your spare time?"

"Spare time?" Again with the eyes. "Are you serious?"

"You know what I mean. What do you do all day? With all that power and knowledge you could do anything you wanted to. You could build stars, play with the laws of nature like they were Lincoln Logs, try bungee jumping . . ."

"Yeah, I *could* if I *wanted* to, but you are forgetting one thing: Just because I'm omniscient, omnipotent, and omnipresent doesn't mean I have om-bition. I've experienced everything there is to experience and done everything there is to do an infinite number of times over and will continue to do so forever. Bungee jumping?! Give me a break."

"So what do you *do*? Just sit there?"

"We OBOE are really only good for one thing."

"Oh, what's that?"

"We narrate."

"You narrate?"

"Yeah, we narrate—everything. We know everything that is going on and we happen to be blessed with low baritone sax, movie-trailer voices perfect for voice-overs, so we narrate. You know that voice you hear sometimes in your head, filling you in on all the stuff that is plainly obvious?"

"You mean like the voice that I use to talk to myself inside my own head when I'm thinking about something?"

"That's the one."

"You mean, that isn't *me* talking to myself?"

"Nope. That's us."

"But what about all the times I think about stupid shit. How can that be the voice of all-knowing reason?"

"What do you want me to say? Sometimes we just like to fuck with you guys."

XI

THE MAN UPSTAIRS

"The Man Upstairs will see you now, Mr. Stanford."

"Actually, Stanford is my first name."

"Oh, did you actually go to college?"

"No, I just ate the meat pies, like everyone else."

"Well, I wouldn't worry too much about that Mr. . . ."

"Adam. Stanford Adam."

"I wouldn't worry about that, Mr. Adam. I haven't met anyone who went to school the old-fashioned way for a long time. But the pies are just as good. It all makes you money in the end, now doesn't it?"

"I was a history major."

"Oh, dear."

• • •

ticka-ticka-ticka-ticka-ticka-ticka-ticka . . .

• • •

STAN FOUND himself in the middle of a conversation. For most people, discovering themselves in the middle of a conversation without a clue as to when or how it started would be a bit jarring, but for Stan it was how he began the majority of his weekdays. Best to just take it in stride and play along. He also found himself reading last January's issue of *Snakes & Woodworking* magazine and peering over the glossy centerfold. Ten feet in front of him was an ornately carved white marble desk decorated with two cheap, shallow, white plastic baskets designed to sequester 8 and 1/2" by 11" sheets of paper, titled "IN" and "OUT." A typewriter and an old touch tone-dial with big red buttons were the only other accessories. The buttons *kachunked* like an ailing 8-track player when they were punched. A name plate at the head of the desk read "Doris."

Top-heavy and wearing a beehive and a low-cut white dress, Doris was filing her nails with a tongue depressor. Behind her was a thirty-foot mural of heavenly Sweetness—Walter Payton. In between the desk and the nondescript folding chair supporting Stan's backside was a strip of loud Studio 54 carpeting—the kind only left behind in bowling alleys and old movie theaters. A glance left and right revealed nothing. Aside from Doris, Sweetness, the desk, and the carpet, the "room" had no conceivable walls, windows, or ceiling of any kind.

Neither were there conceivable pants swaddling his exposed legs, although he did still have his shoes. And his

Mardi Gras rosary. Beyond that, the entire environment was altogether foreign to him. The last thing he recalled was Kevin rolling double sixes on a backgammon board, jogging in place atop a VW Golf floating in an ocean of Lucky Charms, himself fully clothed and confused. Something had clearly transpired between then and now. Some detective work was in order.

"And who exactly is *he*?" inquired Stan.

"*He,*" said the receptionist, rolling her eyes "is the Man Upstairs and He doesn't like to be kept waiting. So I suggest you get moving before you put Him behind schedule. No telling what might happen. Believe me, you don't want to be around Him when He's in a state."

"All right, all right. Where is this . . . Man Upstairs?"

"Upstairs. First door on your right."

Getting information from this woman was like trying to read Chinese underwater. Stan figured the best way to get his pants back was to forge ahead and take his chances with this Man Upstairs, whoever he might be.

• • •

What Stan was unaware of at that moment was that he, along with his sister, had been dropped off moments earlier by his new flame, Wanda, having just been pulled like quantum taffy through space-time at the speed of darkness. Having traveled an unquantifiable distance in what was in actuality no time flat, his brain was understandably jarred. Unaware of his surroundings while his mind was rebooting,

Stan was sat down in a chair and given a magazine to pass the time as he waited to see Wanda's boss for some reason pertaining to the church. Lulu, whose mind was running a much faster operating system than her brother's, took only a second to come to. Realizing that Stan might take a while to awaken from his stupor, Wanda had decided to take Lulu on the dime tour while they waited for Stan to stop drooling. Thus, Stan was left to face the Man Upstairs ill-equipped in foreknowledge, companionship, or proper attire.

• • •

At the top of the stairs were an Olympian set of heavy French doors. Stan straightened his rosary and made sure that his boxer shorts still left something to the imagination. First impressions are the most important; and they were seldom made well with your bits and bobs flopping about like a trout on a trampoline—unless you were in Vegas, where stuff like that really wasn't a big deal. Stan turned the knob of the polished handle and cautiously opened the door just wide enough to squeeze his voice through.

"Ahem. Excuse me. Is anyone there?" He poked his head slowly through the widening crack in the door. "I was told there was a . . . well—er—a Mr. Man Upstairs who I could find here that wanted to see me," whispered Stan.

"Come in, come in. No time to stand around. We've got to get right to work. No t—Good gracious, man! Where are your pants?!"

Stan began spluttering like a cotton gin. "Er—hello, sir—um—my name is Sta—"

"Your pants, man! You've forgotten your pants!"

"Well—er—sir, I didn't forget them, exactly. I just don't seem to have them at this present moment."

This fact vexed Stan. Finding yourself underdressed below the waist was not all that uncommon for one in his line of work—drunk or clergyman,* take your pick—but he was positive that he had been fully clothed just a few moments prior. Pants aren't in the habit of getting up and walking away unless they are filled with legs of the moving variety, and Stan's legs were clearly standing right beneath him. He tried to think on the matter but instead heard only a low movie-theater voice ruminating about his mind: *Sometimes we just like to fuck with you guys.*

"Where are they? You can't be walking around without your pants. No one will take you seriously; this isn't Vegas. It's not proper protocol. No siree, not proper at all."

"Well that's just the thing, sir. I wasn't exactly expecting to be in any meeting."

"I should think not. You can't do very much of anything dressed like that. It's the first rule of getting things done: Make sure you are wearing pants!"

"Yes, sir. Of course, sir. I apologize. Very sorry."

· · ·

---

* Concealing robes are well-documented to promote all manner of sartorial shenanigans.

Stan was talking to an exact replica of Paul Newman on his 80th birthday, except for the fact that he had a beard as long as a '49er's and didn't look quite as angry all the time. He wore a dashing gray suit and expensive Italian leather shoes. The unmistakable impression of wealth fulminated in the balmy office air. It smelled like fresh poppy-seed bagels and Old Spice.

The office was lavishly furnished with a plush, cream-colored leather sofa, a hand-blown coffee table, and a stock ticker. The stock ticker played music that went like this:

ticka-ticka-ticka-ticka-ticka-ticka-ticka . . .

The only person who could hear the music was the man in the gray suit and the '49er beard. By simply shifting his money around as one would furniture, he was able to cultivate wealth like sugar cane. Listening to his money reproduce like bunny rabbits was music to his ears. To everyone else it sounded like a typewriter fugue.

ticka-ticka-ticka-ticka-ticka-ticka-ticka . . .

"Well, come in. Come in. We haven't got all day you know. There is a lot to do around here and precious little time to be farting around, so let's get down to business. Would you care for some refreshment?"

"No, thank you, sir."

"Doris, some tea, please," he ordered into the intercom, "and some pants for Mr. Adam here. Drawstring will do. That way we don't have be fussed about the size."

Before his finger had even been lifted from the inter-com, Doris was entering the room with a tray of tea and biscuits and the bottom half of a surgeon's gown. As she poured two cups of Lady Grey, Stan slipped on the draw-string trousers.

"Thank you, Doris. That'll be all for now. Please hold all my calls until we are done." He motioned for Stan to take a seat and help himself to a cup. "I imagine you are probably wondering exactly where you are right now."

"Well, yes sir, that thought had crossed my mind," said Stan.

"Yeah, they all have that look on their faces when they first get here."

"Excuse me, sir, but who exactly are *they* and where just precisely is *here*?"

"My, you are an inquisitive one, Mr. Adam."

"How do you know my name?"

"Again with the questions. Don't you let anyone else get a word in?"

"Well—"

"How do you expect the conversation to go anywhere with you rifling off queries willy-nilly? This isn't *Jeopardy*, you know."

"Well—uh—I don't know, sir."

"Good. That's how we like to keep it up here."

"Yes, but—wha—am I—"

"My name is Sheldon. I run things around here," he said as he juiced the pulp out of Stan's hand. "I'm not going to lie to you, Stan. Things are not looking good. No siree, things have really gone down the shitter. We need to move fast, Stan, you and I. We really have to boogie if we are going to get on top of this thing."

"Yes, sir, Mr. Sheldon. I should think you're right."

"Actually, Sheldon in my first name."

"Very sorry Mister . . ."

"In order for you to pronounce it correctly we would have to install an extra temporal lobe in that brain of yours. I still don't know how you guys walk around with those things. It amazes me you can get anything done at all. We don't have time to go into it all, but suffice it to say if I told you my last name as you are constituted now, you would hemorrhage on the spot. And we certainly can't have that, now can we?"

"I would prefer to avoid a brain hemorrhage, sir. That's very kind of you, Mr.—er—Sh—"

"Plain old Shelly will do. You can dispense with all this mister nonsense. We're all working together now, wouldn't you say so, Stan?"

"Uh—yes, all together, sir."

"Shelly."

"I mean Shelly."

"That's the spirit. I knew you would be the right man for the job."

It became apparent to Stan that he was being considered for some type of employment position. He had been to job interviews before, but none of them had gotten past the waist-down naked introduction stage. Now that things had progressed on to the interviewing portion of the interview, he was in uncharted waters. The situation was delicate.

"And the job, I'm sure would be right for me, Shelly, if I knew what it was." Stan braced himself. He was not sure if what he had just said was a question.

"Well, you would do what you've been doing, but with our help, obviously. You should've piped up sooner, Stan. We had no idea things had gotten so bad. I mean, we knew about the Buddhists and everything—"

"The Buddhists, sir?"

"Was that a question?"

"No, sir. Just . . . clarifying." Shelly gave him a scrutinizing squint.

"Yes, the Buddhists and their circle-of-life, reincarnation bologna—"

"Bologna?"

"I couldn't agree more. It's complete bullshit. They're all Stalinists, if you ask me."

"Stalin, sir? As in Joseph?"

"Red, commie, Buddhist bastards. Don't get me started."

"Yes, sir."

"But like I said, we knew all about the Buddhists and that damned traitor Churlborough. But it wasn't until Agent Wanda—"

"Wanda, sir?"

"Agent Wanda, my daughter—"

"Your *daughter?!*" guffawed Stan, percolating the clarification through his Lady Grey.

"My daughter. Blonde, beautiful, brilliant. I know you two met. She told me all about it."

"She told you *all* about it?"

"She sure did. Has nothing but the highest praise for you, Stan."

"She does?" Stan's ventricles were doing the jitterbug. She wouldn't have told him about *that*, would she have? "But she said she was an insurance agent."

"She *is* an insurance agent. We all are. What do you think you are doing in the office of the CEO of the largest insurance company in the Universe?"

"You guys sell life insurance?"

Shelly just stared back at him incredulously. "Why in creation would we want to insure something as silly and profitless as life?"

• • •

Humans are a notoriously careless species. It has nothing to do with genitals, either. Sex or not, humans from any planet will rampage through everyday life like a speed demon with cataracts, heedless to all impending danger. They are a race of daredevils.

On a daily basis, humans voluntarily seal themselves inside four-wheeled petroleum bombs for no other purpose than to hone their obscenity-yelling skills. To increase the risk, they insist on whizzing these explosive conveyances blithely from one location to the next at breakneck speeds, confident that they will be saved from bodily harm by a wispy lap belt and a balloon stuffed into the steering wheel. They spend an average of twenty-three and a half hours a day microwaving their intellects in front of anti-creativity screens, persist on flying through the atmosphere on hunks of less-than-volant steel, legalized the consumption of mood-altering poisons, and base their most important life choices on information gleaned from "news" channels. Humans are really nothing more than hotdogging stuntmen whose preference for reckless abandon borderlines on psychosis. They are the appendix of the Universe; there really is no conceivable reason for them to be around anymore.

Amazingly, this helter-skelter mentality is not a result of stupidity, although humans certainly have enough of that to go around. It is instead a remnant of a natural defense mechanism which was physically purged from the human genome eons ago by evolution, but whose psychological residue still manifests itself in the species to this very day.

It all harkens back to a time very early in human development—way before the monkeys. Then, like now, human brains were haphazardly located in the head, flailing out in the open like a parade marshal. This was also well before evolution had deduced that it might be prudent to envelope the most important organ in the human body within a hard, protective skull. Brains jiggled atop human necks like jello molds, protected by nothing but a thin layer of fatty tissue and a mop of hair.

The number one predator of humans at the time was the Great Woolly Wildebear Rex, the savage ancestral missing link between Sasquatch and the anteater. Standing at eight feet tall, the Great Woolly Wildebear Rex was equipped by Mother Nature with a three-foot snout designed for a single, sinister purpose: sucking human brains out their skull-less heads like they were root-beer floats. To the Great Woolly Wildebear Rex human brains were like medical-grade ambrosia, a narcotic delicacy they would stop at nothing to obtain. Generation after generation, these savage creatures hunted Man to the brink of extinction for want of his savory cerebral caviar—even though they could have cared less about the rest of the body. Humans are really very stringy and gamey. Not much you can do with them but slow cook them on low heat for the afternoon with a little rosemary and keep your fingers crossed. The Great Woolly Wildebear Rex didn't have any rosemary.

It is worth pointing out that humans were also much more athletic and flexible back then. Remember that this was well before the remote control was invented, so these humans of yore bore little resemblance to the atrophied lumps of tissue that populate recliners and couches throughout the Universe of today. Back then, humans bounced around like bendy gazelles; they were quite evasive. But it wasn't enough to keep their brains from being snacked on by their insatiable adversary. In the end, it was the thinking that was doing them in.

Woefully unprotected as it was, the human brain *was* pretty large and, as a result, humans found themselves, more and more, just sitting there contemplating a whole range of juicy little brain teasers which had previously not occurred to them. Questions like: *I wonder what this does?, What would happen if I did such and such?,* and *What could I possibly do to get rid of those damned Great Woolly Wildebear Rex?* kept on popping up out of the blue. And when they did, Man sat down to think them over. This was when the Wildebear Rex pounced.

The entire race was about to throw in the towel—only a mere handful remained—when a shrewd young gentleman invented the most ingenious method for using his noodle without losing his brain. Any time he wanted to get some thinking done he would just hide his malleable head in his rear end. The Head Up Your Ass Defense caught on like napalm, and it wasn't long before the entire population was getting all their thinking done with their heads lodged snugly inside their impregnable posteriors. Without a brain exposed to feast on, the Great Woolly Wildebear Rex eventually gave up on humans and moved on to ants.

This, of course, did not happen overnight, but rather over millennia of continuous rump refuge—and not without side effects for human reasoning. Thinking with your head up your ass may be a wonderful deterrent to debrainification, but it doesn't really help much in the way of cogitating properly. The end result was mankind's inability to grasp the macabre irresponsibility of living every day like Evel Knievel. Even after skulls came along and made it physically impractical to stick one's head inside one's own ass, most of the race still, as a subconscious reflex, did the majority of their thinking up there. In the end, more humans would die from criminal disregard for safety no-brainers like gravity or the anti-health benefits of ingesting double quarter-pound aggregate meat-substitute patties warmed in imitation animal lipids, wrapped with processed cheese and salted like a Carthaginian plot of real estate, than having their brains slurped out by the Great Woolly Wilde-bear Rex.

• • •

It doesn't take a Harvard MBA to realize that such pro-digious death rates open the door to a lucrative insurance market for the bounty of bodiless souls that are left over. Afterlife Inc. was soon founded, and it wasn't long before they were the largest provider of afterlife insurance in the Universe.

"You know you're going to die, sooner or later—most likely sooner. Just give us all your time, money, attention, and devotion, and we'll make sure your soul gets to where it ought to be. Just sign here, please."

"What about all this fine print here at the bottom? What does that say?"

"Oh, I wouldn't worry about that."

XII

POLICY

"I don't see what the big deal is."

"You don't see what the big deal is?! Is that supposed to be a joke, Mr. Miller? Do you see me laughing?"

"It's not as if they're illegal. You can get them anywhere. Half the time they give them away for free."

"The same can be said for bad advice and venereal diseases."

"Why do you think I used them in the first place?"

• • •

*P*LEASE HAVE *Your Policies Ready* read the signs placed every fifty feet along the serpentine queue. Gumballs was uncertain how long he had been in line, but he was reasonably sure that the Olympics had come and gone numerous times. There were no clocks, though, so it was really anybody's guess. An eternity had passed in the waiting room. He had watched as the number of every associate around his table was gradually called, prompting their release, only for a new disoriented occupant to *pft* into the empty seat a moment later. The only thing that didn't change were the magazines and the Kenny G. After his good friend Pumpernickel had been called away, he had tried to commit suicide by paper cut, but the magazines were much too old and overly molested to do anything other than irritate his skin. It had only served to anger the staff and get him sent back to the beginning. When his number had finally been called he felt giddier than a prom-night virgin.

The waiting room had been heaven compared to this place, though. At least there were magazines. All he had to read now where the maddening signs that cropped up every fifty feet or so in a line that lumbered into the horizon. Ceaseless. He tried to flag down an orderly that was hustling by.

"Excuse me, Miss."

"What is it, grandpa? Can't you see I'm busy here."

"Sorry to bother you, but I don't understand the signs."

"What's not to understand? Just have your policy in hand when you get to the front. We can't afford to have people shuffling through their pockets like Columbo when the time comes. Got to keep the line moving. And whatever you do, *don't* lose it!"

"Yeah, but what is this policy they're talking about?"

"Your insurance policy."

"But I don't have an insurance policy."

"*Everyone* has a policy. You wouldn't be here if you didn't. And we never make mistakes."

"What policy?"

"How should I know? Just check your breast pocket."

• • •

Breast pockets were an enigma. They had been and would forever baffle anthropologists and fashioneers alike. They served no clear purpose, yet one could scarcely wander a few steps out their front door without running into one—not that you minded running into them. Something about breast pockets mesmerized and comforted the human race. They were like guns; just knowing that they were there made everyone sleep better at night. No one could explain why, but humans were helpless to make a shirt without one. Having an un-pocketed breast was like eating a burger with a knife and fork; it just looked queer.

"Hey, what do you think of my new polo shirt?"

"Ooooh! I especially like this little breast pocket. It's so small and entirely useless."

"I know. Isn't it just the best?"

This predilection for breast pockets actually manifested itself on the sub-atomic—that is to say, spiritual—level. Buried deep within the mitochondrial DNA of every human was the innate requirement to manufacture shirts decorated with breast pockets, hanging off their bosoms like Cinco de

Mayo decorations, no matter how pointless they appeared. They had no earthly reason to be there.

Their existence was of an entirely unearthly nature. Humans needed them to house and protect their insurance policies through the harrowing wait for the journey into the afterlife.

• • •

"Show me a man who uses his breast pocket to house anything but nitrogen and I'll show you an honest tax return," protested Gumballs. "Everyone knows they are about as useful as Esperanto. I just like the way—" He stopped as he put his hand over his heart. There *was* something in there. He reached in and pulled it out.

Gumballs stared at his insurance policy for a moment, nonplussed. It was small, no bigger than his thumb. He had seen it before. His grandmother had given him this very same object back when he was just a lad, right before she passed. Could she have been involved in this insurance scheme, too?

Staring straight back at him was a one-inch figurine of a man nailed to a Roman torture device. What was his name again?

• • •

His mother had once told Gumballs that good things come to those who wait. She had forgotten to add the all-important modifier "eventually" to her little nugget of wisdom. By his estimation he had now spent at least twice as long waiting post-death—first in the waiting room and now in this never-ending line—as he had spent living pre-death. In that time he had developed an important insight into waiting: If you are ever to wait in line for just short of eternity, it is best to wait behind a person who is wearing something interesting enough to keep you occupied, or at the very least, something lacking the stupidity to unhinge your sanity. Soft pastels are good as long as there are no horizontal lines. Avoid anything with food or pretty girls unless it is being worn by pretty girls with food to share. Writing of any kind can be catastrophic. Shirts that display clever little comic quips like *Rocker Spocker Shocker* or *I Put the Sexy in Dumbass*—although appearing harmless enough at first glance, perhaps even inciting a chuckle or two—will turn your brain to vegetable pilaff after eyeballing them for the equivalent of a few lifetimes. In Gumballs's case, he was fated to stare down the back of an Andy Warhol T-shirt. After lifetimes transfixed in contemplation, Gumballs still didn't get it.

In the end, though, Mommy is always right, and Gumballs's was no exception. At first it was nothing more than a polyp on the horizon, but as Gumballs inched closer there could be no doubt. He was coming up on a gate.

• • •

There is a myth which managed to worm itself into Earth-lore long ago. For as long as anyone can remember, the idea that the end point of the conveyer belt of life was guarded by a sentry of pearly white gates had been propagated throughout every tale and legend since Gilgamesh was in diapers. In point of fact, this is a complete fallacy. The whole cockamamie story is just an ingenious marketing ploy used to rob unwitting customers out of their hard-earned money. For much the same reason that people spend oodles of cash on destroying relationships every Valentine's Day,* or the Japanese line up around the block on Christmas to buy Kentucky Fried Chicken,† pearl salesman have disseminated the fable for eons in order to drive up the price of the little ivory beads.

"Get your pearl necklaces here! Get 'em while they're hot!"

"Egad, man! Do you know how much you're asking for this?! I could buy half of New Jersey at this price!"

"Why in heaven's name would you want to do that?"

"You make a good point—but this price is outrageous!"

"They didn't make the Gates of Paradise out of breakfast pastries, now did they?"

"Well   er—no, I suppose not—"

"*Or* out of Egyptian cotton. Am I right?"

"I hear you."

---

* See: *This Valentine's Gift Is Not as Good as My Best Friend's* by Everyday Girlfriend or *Whose Idea Was It to Entitle Every Woman on the Planet to a Gift All on the Same Day?* by Male Lament.

† If you haven't ordered a week in advance don't even bother queuing up—really.

"I should hope you do. The Gates of Valhalla are not just regular ole hum-drum white. They could have made them out of adobe plaster, or cream cheese, or non-recycled paper—but they didn't. They made them out of—"

"All right, all right. You've made your point. I'll take two."

The gates are not pearly white. They are actually a drab tranquilizer gray that has faded into a dispiriting Tokyo-during-the-day taupe. There is very little majestic about them. In fact, there is no "them" at all. There is only one gate—one single subway turnstile which was grifted off the New York City Metropolitan Transit Authority for next to nothing at a city auction in 1981. A few dings and dents aside, the gate works perfectly fine.

A gruff security guard with a black bobby helmet and a billy club stands vigil. His name tag says "You Don't Want To Mess With Me," and he is the last line of defense against unsavory brigands gate-jumping their way to the Promise Land. The first line of defense comes in the form of an elderly card table sat at by a rickety old woman in a folding chair. Her name tag says "Mrs. G." You don't want to mess with her, either.

One by one, the applicants stepped up to the table and rigidly displayed their credentials in military fashion. Mrs. G would accept the orange slip, scrutinize it briefly before adding it to a swollen heap of orange sprawl behind her, briefly run her pencil over the clipboard in her hands, tick a box at the bottom of the page, and finally finish off the entire maneuver by motioning for the next prospective entrant to step forward. The whole process, the one for which Gumballs had been waiting the better part of eternity to come to pass, lasted an average of four seconds. Gumballs watched the procedure unfold a dozen times as the line in front of him gradually dwindled to zero.

Xanadu.

• • •

"Please present your policy."

"Gladly," said Gumballs, hardly able to contain his excitement as he handed over the little figurine. He was actually going to make it over to the Other Side. "I hope you don't mind me saying, Miss, but I—we—everyone, I mean—we have been waiting for quite a while. Don't you think it might go a bit faster if you had another turnstile?"

"I suppose you also want to complain that it isn't made of pearl, now don't you?" Mrs. G was not amused. Who could blame her? Doing a job where you are constantly reminded of the utterly endless nature of the less-than-exhilarating task that is your charge—by, for example, a never-ending line extending hopelessly before you into infinity—causes venom to build up in your molars like bad jokes. Without a coffee break to empty the poison, the venom gets transmitted via the carrier's voice, just like all sexually transmitted diseases. This is why kissing a grocery bagger or Department of Motor Vehicles employee within an hour of finishing his or her shift can be fatal. "Why not just have me standing here in a lei and a coconut bikini ready to give every slob who rolls in a welcome hummer, while we're at it? You'd like that, wouldn't you? This is Paradise, Mr. Miller—not Hawaii."

Sexual gratification from this woman was the furthest thing from his mind.

"I was just saying—"

"We *had* two turnstiles way back when. Couldn't stop you lot from jumpin' 'em every time Pete, here, turned around to tie his shoe." She motioned her head toward the burly constabulary figure guarding the gate. "No, sir, one is all we can do."

Gumballs had heard enough. He did not want to get into a tiff with this hag, not with the Happy Hunting Ground lying just beyond the heavenly turnstile. He moved toward the gate but was halted by the hulking security guard.

"Mrs. Granderson is callin' you back, buddy. Looks like there is a problem with your paperwork."

"Mr. Miller! Just where do you expect you are going?" It was the voice only an 8th grade English teacher could muster while trying to get the the average student to explain why he or she had used the past indicative where the situation clearly called for present subjunctive. Retired banshees are the only other beings known to be able to produce such terrifying inflection.

"I was just—"

"Sit down, Mr. Miller! You've been flagged!"

"Flagged? What does that mean?"

"It means there is problem."

"Problem? How is that possible? I have insurance."

"You may have *insurance*, Mr. Miller, but that doesn't *ensure* anything."

"But everyone else—"

"Everyone *else* was keen enough to have taken out a policy with much more liberal coverage than you."

"What are you saying? These people are all Scandinavian?"

"You see these little orange slips here?" She pointed to the mountain of Halloween amassed behind her. "These will ensure you a ticket to Paradise as long as you follow the rule on the front. The policy is very straightforward." Gumballs was well versed in the Chadic faith and their Bohemian methods—very pleasant people, although the fact that you couldn't get anything done without first undressing was, on occasion, a bit of a nuisance. "You don't have one of these, Mr. Miller, now do you?" she chided as the corners of her mouth perked upwards derisively. "Your policy is much more, how shall we say . . . nuanced."

She then placed the figurine of the man on the Roman torture device on the table in front of Gumballs. What was his name again?

"Don't get many of these policies anymore. Going to have to take a little gander at your file," she gloated. "If you would please follow me, Mr. Miller, you will have to be probed further."

"Probed? What on Earth do you mean?" This incited a chuckle from the old woman.

"Earth? Just where do you think you are, Mr. Miller? Come along now. You and I will be getting to know each other a little better."

"Now wait just a plum-pickin' minute! What is the meaning of this? I demand to—" Gumballs's protests were cut short by a pair of gorillas wearing black bobby helmets, accosting him from behind and persuading him to accompany them off to the side by reminding his rotator cuffs that they experience far less pain when they are well situated snug in their sockets like good little joints. These gentlemen wore name tags that said "I Told You Not To Mess With Us" and "Jake."

Gumballs soon found himself in what appeared to be an interrogation chamber—a nondescript concrete room lacking any decoration except for a door on one wall, a dressing-room mirror on the other, and Kenny G saturating the air like mustard gas. A sterile public-employee break-room table anchored the center of the room; and anchored to it, via a pair of handcuffs, was Gumballs—feeling slightly unsettled. The last time he had been handcuffed and probed was while waiting for an international flight. A St. Patrick's Day layover at O'Hare and a bar full of National Rifle Association delegates had resulted in a few new friends and one hell of a carpet burn. That had been a hoot. This room and these people, on the other hand, gave him the heeby-jeebies.

Mrs. G entered the room—now sporting a pair of black Oakleys despite the fact that the room was completely dark except for a single naked light bulb above the table swinging like a Key West Tupperware party—and thwumped down a manilla folder that could have moonlighted as the unabridged Courier New version of *War and Peace*. A plume of dust mushroomed portentously into the air.

Gumballs did not care for his current situation. He could feel his fortunes turning like leftover sushi. Calculating his chances of getting past this woman by using Jeeve's Law for Determining How Bad the Contents of That File Are Going to Sting—thickness times dust over regrettably asinine comments previously uttered squared—he braced himself for impact.

"When was the last time you had confession?"

"Confession? For what? Am I under arrest?"

"I see," was Mrs. Granderson's response. It was not the type of "I see" that flops out after solving an algebraic equation. It was more along the lines of the "I see" you get from a Spanish inquisitor who is blind. She made a note in the margin. "Says here that there was a little incident while on a combat tour in Southeast Asia. Care to say anything about *that*, Mr. Miller?"

"You talkin' about that night me and Alfalfa Roberts where trapped in that elevator for sixteen hours with nothing but a case of merlot to pass the time?"

"Do you deny it, sir?"

"What's there to deny? We were young, drunk, and bored. Is that a crime? To tell you the truth, it wasn't as good as I thought it would be."

"It says here you also used a condom."

"Hell yeah. We may have been young, drunk, and bored, but we weren't *stupid.*"

The old lady chortled like an overconfident super villain. "I don't think I have to remind you, Mr. Miller, that your particular policy doesn't cover contraceptives."

"Contra-what?"

"Anything that would prevent you from 'making a baby' *au naturel.*"

"*Baby*?! I was having sex with a *man.* "

"Please be advised that anything you say can be used against you, Mr. Miller."

"I want a lawyer!"

. . .

There are certain lawyers who inspire confidence in their clients. They dress sharp, talk slick, and above all, wear unlikability like a mink coat. All the best ones are draped in it. The biggest douche bags always make the best lawyers. They are the ones who are able to set aside the natural human tendency to do what is not abhorrent by insulating themselves from potentially ruinous remorse with justice and obscenely high hourly rates. They are then able to turn around and buy all the friends they need. Nothing turns an unlikable jackass into the most popular guy in the room like a wallet full of Benjaminian mojo.

This is not to say that there are not a great many litigators who are stand-up individuals; quite the contrary. A majority of solicitors throw great summer barbecues which are happily attended, pro bono, by multitudes of co-workers and acquaintances. They toss Lawn Jarts, sip margaritas, and happily play the role of benevolent host, doling out affable praise to their neighbors as magnanimous lords of geniality. These are the type of lawyers anyone among us would count him- or herself lucky to befriend—just as long as they are not representing us in any sort of legal capacity.

Find yourself being represented by a nice guy and you might as well pony up the settlement on the spot and save yourself some time and aggravation. When you find yourself in a real jam, the smart money—copious amounts of it—is on the biggest jerk you can find. Justice is a dish best served supercilious.

• • •

Gumballs's lawyer was the nicest guy he had ever dreamt of meeting. Squeezed comically into an undersized bowling shirt festooned with Hawaii and sucked tight against his torso, buttons quivering with fatigue as they endeavored to prevent the shirt from rupturing into tatters, his ensemble resembled that of a B-list superhero sidekick's. Steady work had not been readily available for the Incredible Bulk, so he had instead turned to a life in the Public

Defender's Office to put bread on the table. In retrospect, he probably shouldn't have substituted his low-carb diet for cable TV—or at the very least bought a bigger shirt. He wore the baseball cap of his son's Little League team—of which he was the coach—and always carried around pictures of his beautiful family, which he distributed like parade candy to everyone he met. His wife made the best lemon meringue pie in the county. Worse, he smelled of hot dogs and margaritas and came armed with only a legal pad and a Lawn Jart—the lame, safety type that skip out of the yellow circle like Mexican beans, not the javelin-esque original which might have proven to be a useful weapon in a tight spot like this.

"Sorry to have kept you waiting, Mr. Miller. Was having a little barbecue on the home front when I got the call. It is a pleasure to meet you, though. My friends—and my clients—call me Stu." Stu extended his hand jovially. "Brought you a hot dog and a drink. Hope you don't mind light beer. I can always go and get you something else if you like." Gumballs accepted the handshake dejectedly.

"No, this will do fine. Thanks, Stu."

"Oh, think nothing of it. And be sure to save some room for dessert. My wife sent along a piece of her lemon meringue pie—best in the county, you know." Gumballs's heart capsized. This guy was probably on a first name basis with his IRS agent. "Would you like to see some pictures of my family?"

"I would love to, Stu, but perhaps another time—when I'm not in such a bind. I kind of have a few other things to worry about at the moment."

"Quite right. You're quite right. Very sorry about that. Sometimes I can get a little carried away, I know. Let's talk about your case and see if we can't help you out."

"Thank you, Stu."

"They tell me you were flagged? Is that right?"

"I think so. That's what Mrs. G said, anyway."

"Why don't you go ahead and tell me everything that happened. Don't leave anything out. I can't help you unless I know exactly what went down." He discarded his Lawn Jart and produced the legal pad.

"There really isn't much to tell. I waited in line like everyone else, got to the front, presented my policy when asked, and before I knew it I was chained to this table here and being grilled by the old lady. She had a manilla folder."

"Okay. Let's back up for a second. When you handed over your orange pamphlet, was it damaged in any way? Perhaps a dog-ear or a coffee stain?"

"My policy wasn't orange."

"Not orange?" Stu repeated, confused. "What do you mean it wasn't orange?"

"I mean I had a different policy than everyone else."

"What kind did you have?"

Gumballs pulled out his policy put it on the table.

Stu blanched. "Oh, dear. I'm afraid this complicates things a bit."

• • •

Misgiving had slide-stepped into timorous consterna-
tion. And forget about botheration; it was now but a
diminutive blip in the rear-view mirror. Stu had been gone
for hours, supposedly negotiating some type of plea bargain
with Mrs. Granderson, but Gumballs was beginning to
think that maybe he had just abandoned ship. The second
he had gotten a glimpse of the policy, his chipper outlook
soured considerably, thereafter speaking only in guttural
sobs. When he finally stopped the crying, he began vomit-
ing. The hot dogs were not sitting very well anymore.

That had been ages ago, though, and Gumballs's hope
of ever escaping this soprano-sax torture box began to fade.
He had all but given up hope when Stu entered the room,
shoulders slumped.

"Gumballs—"

"Stu! You're back! I was beginning to think you had left
me here."

"Sorry. I've been going toe to toe with Mrs. Granderson."

"So? How did it go?"

"Well . . . you'd better sit down."

"I am sitting down. That's all I've been doing for the
last who knows how many hours."

"Oh—right. Well, then I suppose *I* should sit down."
He eased into his folding chair like a defeated general into a
bath of scalding reparations. "Well . . . there is some good
news . . ."

"Yes, that's good."

"I was able to get you off for that little transgression involving Mr. Roberts on account of the extenuating circumstances."

"Extenuating circumstances?"

"Yeah, lucky for you, Alfalfa Roberts was an ordained member of the clergy so they are willing to look the other way on that one."

"That's great! Does that mean I'm getting out of here?"

"Well . . . not exactly. I tried my best. I really did. You have to believe me. I pointed out how righteous of a life you had lived; how you hardly ever cheated on your taxes; how you were never arrested, never even had a speeding ticket—"

"And?"

"—how you started a business to help old ladies cross the street safely, how you gave blood once a year, built eighty-seven homes for the less fortunate with your bare hands, saved the life of a nine-year-old boy you had never even met by donating your heart to him—"

"And?"

"—how you said hello to everyone you met, always gave the best birthday presents, never once uttered a curse word, invented soup kitchens, re-invented whales—"

"And?"

"—how you never ran for public office, always finished your vegetables, never let your eyes get bigger than your stomach, listened to classical music, took a bite out of crime, and how you were voted Most Likely To Be Considered A Shoo-In By The Almighty When The Time Finally Came by your high school peers—"

"But?"

"—but I'm afraid there are still 47,685 violations of the terms of agreement for your particular insurance policy."

"Violations?"

"Yes. Most of them have to do with you—er—taking matters into your own hands . . . you know . . . when there wasn't anybody else—say your wife—around to help you out . . . with matters of that nature."

"*That?! That* is enough to negate an entire lifetime of saintly living?"

"I'm afraid so. There is nothing I can do. The policy is ironclad." Gumballs could not believe what he was hearing. "I might point out that, especially for a man of your age, that number shows a remarkable level of restraint. I've seen guys who have that bested before they can drive."

"So what happens now?"

"I'm afraid your insurance policy is void. They will not admit you past the subway turnstile to Eternal Happiness."

"But where will I go?"

"There is only once place left *to* go, Mr. Miller. I'm very sorry. You're being sent down."

"To the minor leagues?"

"Oh, goodness gracious no—nothing that bad. You're being relegated to Perdition."

XIII

HEMOGLOBIN

"So all these people having insurance with us is a bad thing?"

"Now you're getting it, Stan."

"But isn't that what you do here: insure people?"

"Insure—yes. Cover—no. You'll never make any money if you have to cover every smelly slob who takes out a policy with you. For chrissake, we're not in Cuba."

"Then how do we sell insurance that doesn't require us to provide coverage?"

"Like I said, Stan: More innovation. Less scruples."

• • •

Walk with me, Stan." Shelly took him by the shoulder and led him past the stock ticker toward an intimidating marble vault door. "Follow me. There is something that I would like to show you. Behind this door is the secret to our success here at Afterlife." After a 13-digit key code, a retinal scan, and a questionnaire covering overall security satisfaction, a small slot at eye level slid open to reveal a pair of squinty eyes packaged in darkness.

"Password?"

"Buster, would you stop it already? It's me: Shelly. I'm the only one who ever uses this door. It's connected to my office, for chrissake. Is it really necessary to go through this charade *every* day?"

"Sorry, Boss—if you are indeed who you say you are."

"Oh, come off it, Buster!"

"You know the rules: No password, no entry. I could get fired, you know."

"No, you couldn't because *I'm* the one in charge of—"

"Password?"

"Fine, Fine!" he huffed, exhaling asthmatically and rolling his eyes up into his head. "The password is *mint julep.*"

"Can you reconfirm that, sir? It's difficult to understand you once you've gone into one of your conniptions."

"Conniptions?! I most certainly do n—"

"—The password, sir. Or I'm afraid I'm going to have to call security."

Shelly took a moment to cool down and collect himself. "*Mint. Julep.*"

The mechanisms in the lock clanged to life, and the massive door swung open slowly. Buster stood inside, waiting stoically at attention. He had the look of your average Joe Security Guard—hungry to sit down and itching for lunch.

"Now, that wasn't so hard now was it, sir?"

"Did you have to make me say it twice?"

"You can never be too careful with these things, sir."

Shelly led Stan through the open door. As they stepped over the threshold, Stan felt the austerity in the atmosphere rise. It made his clothes less comfortable.

"Welcome to the Hall of Fame."

Shelly marched Stan down the stately hall. White marble from ceiling to floor and the length of five football fields, the Hall paid homage to the greatest of the great, the creamiest of the crop, the biggest of the kahunas. Parenthetically flanking the left and right side of the Hall like sesame bread on a sideways party sub were two rows of august white marble busts, spaced at five-meter intervals, each portraying the likeness of one of the great insurance salesmen of yore.

"Now these men and women, Stan—these are the people who built the company that you see today. These are the folks who made it all happen. It is times like this, when things are not looking quite so profitable, that I like to take a stroll down this stately avenue to remind myself that selling insurance isn't for the faint of heart. If you want to get ahead you have to get tough: More innovation. Less scruples."

"So all these people . . . sold insurance?"

"These people didn't just sell insurance, Stan—they sold *profitable* insurance. That's the real key. Anyone can sell *insurance*. But only the greats can sell the real shady, duplicitous, reprobate kind."

Stan could not help but feel small in the presence of such great men and women. He listened intently as Shelly outlined the accomplishments of the various salespeople they passed: This guy invented fine print; that gal perfected the art of ignoring guilt. He flim-flammed; she hoodwinked; they duped. And on and on.

"This is all very nice, Shelly. But what does it have to do with me?"

"Because, Stan, if you pull this off, you can bet your bottom dollar that you're going to have your own little statue up here."

"But that's really the only dollar I have left."

"Not to worry, Stan. It will all be taken care of. I've got a good feeling about this. You are going to be the one to save us all."

"But I don't even know what—"

"Hold on to that thought, Stan, my boy. There is just one little thing we've got to take care of first. We need the Board to sign off on you."

• • •

There are two prevailing scales—Celsius and Fahrenheit—used by Earthlings to measure to what degree the particles of a given substance are a-jingling and a-jangling away. Minus-forty just happens to be the magical little entropic quantity at which thermometers calibrated to either scale coalesce into one delightfully conversion-free integer. Minus-forty degrees Fahrenheit is the same as minus-forty degrees Celsius. Scientists have a technical term for this thermal value: *butt cold*. Or to put it in layman's terms: at minus-forty degrees particles are packed tighter than a Tokyo morning subway car, chock-full of jazz musicians, smuggled up a Scotsman's arsehole. You can safely ix-nay any angling-jay. Minus-forty also coincidentally happens to be the temperature of Absolute Profitability—the temperature at which the Great Material Hemoglobin most readily flows through the Universe, enabling the most scrupulous among us to most easily harness its currents and guzzle down the sweet gravy of material success. It is for the latter reason that the Members of the Board of Directors of Afterlife, Inc. see to it that their boardroom is a meat locker. They don't give two shits about Scotsmen's arseholes.

• • •

Stan was completely unaware that minus-forty degrees was such a fantastically remunerative frequency for one's particles to oscillate at. Standing nervously, though, as he was—smack dab in the center of a Wisconsin winter— before an enclave of menacing captains of industry, there were several observations he *did* make about minus-forty degrees: It makes the water vapor in your exhaled breath condense into eco-friendly exhaust fumes; it makes your teeth chatter like the loose foot on your washing machine; and finally—but perhaps most applicable—was the realization that being cloistered away at such an atom-constricting temperature allowed one to understand, clear as properly cooked chicken juice, why wispy little drawstring surgeon's trousers sold about as well as Bermuda shorts in Siberia.

Shelly led the way, Stan playing the role of caboose. "You just let me do all the talking," advised Shelly, discreetly whispering behind himself while maintaining a frontward glance. "The Board can be a pretty tough nut to crack, but I know how to get them to see it my way."

"Your way, Shelly?"

"Quite right, Stan. *Our* way."

"Ah . . . Which way?"

"Distinguished Members of the Board and beloved investors," opened Shelly, addressing the Board Members. "Greetings and salutations from your most humble chief executive officer. I come offering gifts: a solution to the calamitous headache in section eighty-one. Ladies and Gentlemen, fear not. Agent Wanda has, as I assured you she would, performed her duty admirably and brought to us our savior."

A luminescent column of soft white light beamed down on Stan from somewhere up in the rafters, bathing him in brilliance. He was not sure, but he could have sworn that there was a choir stowed under that table, complimenting the light with a five-part major harmony. Remembering Shelly's advice, Stan kept his mouth shut. He presented himself with a graceless curtsey and waited for a response. After a moment of painfully awkward silence, Stan lifted his head to face the soundless music of the Board. Instead of music he received a pungent dress-rehearsal for his gag reflex.

The Directors were all dead—or perhaps alive, depending on how you looked it. Each one sat perched motionless, around the clock, on lofty thrones of chic marble and leather, bejeweled with gaudy ornaments and perfumed with formaldehyde. The formaldehyde and the frigid air helped to keep the smell at bay.

Any group of people who has accumulated as much moolah as the members of this chamber had, could not afford *not* to be hard-wired *at all times* to the comings and goings of their money. This group of savvy investors did not get to their station in life by delegating responsibilities out to salary-requiring subordinates, or by entrusting their fortunes to the greedy hands of the other Members of the Board of Directors with whom they had striven relentlessly to make their great fortune in the first place. Those people were their only friends; they were the last people worthy of trust. Consequently, no one on the Board would risk leaving the chamber, at any moment, for fear of being swindled.

This left the Directors in a bit of pickle: Part ways with their wealth momentarily to perform such trivialities as obtaining sustenance or expelling solid waste from their bodies, or stick it out and rely on profits to nourish them and legal tender to fulfill the absorbency requirements of their diapers. Poorer souls would have tossed in the towel long ago, but these stubborn chieftains of wealth were able to tap into the well-spring of vitality that flows forth from the Almighty Dollar. They had come to understand that an entire existence of worshiping Dollar Almighty—through ritual weekly sacrifices of QT with the family and unwavering devotion to the 24-Karat Rule: *Do unto yourself whatever you think will help that bottom line—laws of Man or decency be damned*—allowed the most faithful to siphon just enough energy from the Great Material Hemoglobin that flows between every dollar, sawbuck, and greenback in the Universe to keep their life force from sinking into bankruptcy. Suckling directly from Dollar Almighty's teat will keep you from expiring indefinitely, sustaining you like the Shackleton diet on heroin. It ain't pretty, though.

From where Stan stood at the head of an antique, oak aircraft-carrier landing strip, he could make out twelve Directors—at least he thought there were twelve, although it could have been a few more or a few less. It was difficult to tell where one ended and the other began. All of them seemed to possess a head, at the very least a fish-bowled brain, each garnished with a monocle and a Cuban cigar. The ones who couldn't smoke directly, whether inhibited by their aq-ranium or constrained by their dearth of respiratory organs, just percolated the smoke through the water filters or ingested the tobacco raw. Gender had waved bye-bye a long time ago. The ones who still had any semblance of a body left over were really not much more than just a mishmash of decaying limbs and quivering organs. Tubes, vents, and durable electrical wiring splayed out at all angles, connecting the Directors to the full regiment of iron lungs, IV drips, kidney dialysis machines, and industrial-strength juicers necessary to supplement the GMH and keep their minds sharp enough to cut the financial mustard. A cacophony of beeps, chirps, and alarms made any attempt to converse within the chamber a knock-down drag-out with an ocean of medical crickets.

Full-time staffs were busy performing the weekly maintenance ritual, feather-dusting plumes of ashen cinders from the Directors into the air momentarily before the shed dermis settled down into its usual sedimentary striations.

The only other person who looked at all healthy, other than Shelly and Stan—although it should be said that "healthy" was not the word people often used to describe Stan's appearance—was an inconspicuous little man located in the corner of the room behind a megalithic book of facts and figures, focused intently on massaging an adding machine and amending the great book. Smart money said he was the Accountant.

"PLEASE STEP FORWARD, MR. STANFORD," boomed the Directors in one collective hive voice.

"Well actually, Stanford is my first—"

"IRRELEVANT. ALL THAT IS RELEVANT IS THAT YOU BELIEVE."

"I'm sorry, bel—"

"DO YOU BELIEVE?!"

"Believe in what?"

"DO YOU BELIEVE IN ONE CURRENCY, THE DOLLAR ALMIGHTY; CREATOR OF ALL MATERIAL BELONGINGS BOUGHT, PURCHASED, OR BORROWED; THROUGH WHICH LUXURY AND OPULENCE ARE MAINTAINED?"

"Er—"

"DO YOU BELIEVE IN THE GREAT MATERIAL HEMOGLOBIN, THE PROVIDER OF PROFITS, THE PURVEYOR OF PLENTITUDE, AND THE RENDERER OF REVENUE?"

"Ah—"

"DO YOU ACKNOWLEDGE ONE MARKET, CONCEIVED IN BRIBERY, AND DEDICATED TO THE PROPOSITION THAT THERE IS NO SUCH THING AS A FREE LUNCH?"

"Well—"

"DO YOU REJECT INSOLVENCY, AND PLEDGE TO STAND READY AT THE BATTLEMENTS OF THE KINGDOM OF GOLD TO DEFEND IT FROM HIS NECESSITOUS, PAUPERIZED MINIONS?"

"Um—"

"CAN YOU BALANCE YOUR CHECKBOOK?"

"Hmmm . . . I write numbers down in it . . . occasionally."

"DO YOU AT LEAST OWN A SWEATER VEST?"

"Uh . . . what about a turtleneck? Will that do?"

"HOW CAN YOU POSSIBLY HELP US MAKE MONEY?"

"Well . . . did I mention I own a church?"

• • •

"So here's what we're going to do, Stan. You're all we've got in section eighty-one, so we're going to have to use you as the foothold."

"The foothold? Sounds dangerous. What does that entail?"

"Nothing more than what you're already doing. And don't worry, I'm sending Wanda along with you. Daughter notwithstanding, she's the best agent I've got. Right now we just need to get some butts in the seats—"

"Pews."

"Pardon?"

"We don't have seats at *Stanford's*. Just pews."

"Pews?"

"Pews. Like benches, only churchier."

"Even better. Now you're thinking with gas, Stan. Pack 'em in like Japanese sardines. Just get some butts in the pews. Once we've established a base of operations, then we can work on expanding. Can't build a church without a cornerstone."

"So basically you just want more people in the bar?"

"Bar?"

"I mean church."

"You mean to tell me that you sell booze at the church? Beyond complimentary sips of wine?"

"Well . . . yes, sir. I meant no dis—"

"Brilliant, Adam! I can't believe no one had thought of that before! Those simple-minded plebs can't keep their grubby mitts off the stuff. Ingenious, Stan! Bravo! I'm going to have to tell the boys to make room for another bust, you keep this up."

"Oh, it's nothing really, sir."

"What about advertising?

"Neon sign."

"Hymns?"

"Jukebox."

"Relic?"

"Disco ball."

"Disco ball?! Fuck willikers! You don't get much more relic than that. Where in the Universe did you manage to unearth one of those?

"Earth. I had the good fortune of being on the original archeological dig of Funkytown."

"You mean to tell me that such a place actually exists? I thought it was just a myth, some leisure-suit legend left over from a bygone era."

"No myth. Would you believe they discovered it right next to Troy? It was a major find at the time. Caused a whole heap of hullabaloo—gave the entire field of anthropology Saturday Night Fever, you know."

"You don't say."

"Oh, yes; very few survived. I was one of the lucky ones."

"Well I'll be damned. It looks like you've got just about all the bases covered. There must be something, Stan— anything. Something that the Company can do to help you get that church of yours thriving? Just name it."

Stan looked up into the eyes of his patron and smiled coyly. He had had an epiphany, of sorts.

"Well . . . there is *one* thing . . ."

XIV

In Flowing Cups

"So how does it work?"

"Just put it up to your mouth, tip, and drink."

"Should I breathe?"

"Only when you're not drinking; otherwise you'll make a mess."

"And then what happens?"

"Then you start to feel better."

"And after that?"

"Rinse and repeat."

"So you're saying all I have to do is drink this, and all my sins are washed away?"

"Well . . . I don't know about that whole 'and now your sins don't really count' business, but I can guarantee you'll be in a better mood."

"Good enough for me. How about these pretzels? What do they do?"

• • •

With Wanda's help and through something nothing short of a miracle, *Stanford's* gradually transformed itself from a hole-in-the-wall money sieve into a hole-in-the-wall blue-chipper. As word spread of the mystical church, business boomed biblically. Pilgrims began to turn up from every corner of the Moon—and after that Earth, Mars, and the whole shebang. The news was out. *Stanford's* was a different kind of church.

There were no hymnals, no incantations, no prayers, no kneeling, no Sunday morning hangover-fests. There were no rituals, no pandering, no pretending, no chastising, no censuring. There were no promises, no finger-wagging, no cover-ups, no flagellating, no pipe organs. There was no bologna. The only thing there was, was something that church-goers had been yearning for ever since ole Saint Pete had first begun flapping his gums. *Stanford's* was the only church with the recipe for Salvation. They sold it on tap.

• • •

"Don't tell me you're at it again, Stan."

"If by 'at it' you mean making brewing history, then you are correct." Stan was in no mood to take any guff from Karl. He was busying himself behind the bar, entangled in a nest of hoses and CO_2 tanks.

"Is this the recipe you got from what's-her-name?"

"Wanda. Her name is Wanda."

"Where is she anyway? Scared her off already? Must have gotten a whiff of your living room."

"She's working. Selling insurance is a tough business, you know. Logs a lot of hours on the road. She said she'd be back to check in on me once I got this new recipe running."

"Sure. She'll be back any second now. Of that I'm positive," jibed Karl in a sing-songy, sarcastic tone.

"What do you know, Karl? It's not as if you've got any women hanging on your arm, now is it? When is the last time you dusted off that pecker of yours?"

Karl erupted in laughter. He was from the American South. Pecker jokes flow like biscuits n' gravy down there. "Ooooeee! Hold up now, before I split my side—you cranky S.O.B." Karl also loved calling people S.O.B.s—not because he was from the American South, though; he just liked the way it rolled off his tongue: *S-O-B*.

"Just you wait and see, Karl. This here is the real deal. I followed the recipe to a tee."

The door opened and in trundled Cramp Holden, smelling of olive loaf and despair. On most days Cramp sauntered about displaying convivial carriage, but today it was obvious that something was saddling his mind.

"Evening Cramp. What can I do you for?"

"You don't happen to have any hemlock back there?"

"Hemlock? Sorry, can't help you there."

"He doesn't have any hemlock, but I'm sure this new brew he's cooked up will do the trick," sniggered Karl as he slapped Cramp on the back entirely too hard. The open-handed back-slap chuckle was the most-used move in Karl's human-contact repertoire. He used it for everything from punchlines to self-defense to indigestion. "What's gotten into you, you sorry S.O.B.?"

"Oh, I don't know. Don't you ever wonder what it's all for, sometimes?" Cramp appeared to be wrestling with a mid-life, existential quandary. Stan witnessed outbursts like these regularly, part of the territory for one who tends bar, but rarely did the symptoms present themselves before the subject tipped a few back. "There I was, just sitting in the deli today, weighing out a pound-and-a-half of German potato salad, when it hit me: Is this all there is to life? Am I doomed to spend the rest of my days doling out pasta salad and slicing cold cuts for the masses? What's the point?"

"There is always a point to life, Cramp," consoled Stan. "What about your family?"

"Dead."

"All of them?"

"Yup. Taken from me by a tainted batch of braun-schweiger at a family reunion back in '07. Would have gotten me, too, if not for the fact that I never touch the stuff. I was the only survivor—the last of my name, the final link of sausage in a long line of deli men dating all the way back to the Salt-Cured Age."

"Braunschweiger, huh? Blimey." Not the most glamor-ous of ways to go out, but who could blame the Holdens? Who doesn't like a good smoked liverwurst stuffed into a fibrous casing? Like pâté, but not so prissy. "Sorry, Cramp. I never knew."

"You are one unlucky S.O.B., I'll give you that."

Karl was about to go for the consoling version of the open-handed back-slap chuckle, but pulled up short after Stan disabled the gesture with a torpedo-eye glare.

"Well, what about your friends?"

Cramp shifted his eyes over to Karl, who was making his daily attempt to break the world record for most desiccated salt cubes stuffed into a single mouth—his mouth—at one time. His face was puckered up like an Eskimo speedo.

"Never mind friends. What about your hobbies?"

"Drinking whiskey count?"

"Interests?"

"None."

"Skills?"

"Nope." Stan had to do something quick before the man broke down and started whimpering like a soccer dandy.

"I know what will cheer you up. Just finished hooking up the brand-new recipe, here." Stan petted the keg as if it were a skittish horse. "Hows about we give her a little test drive?"

"I don't know, Stan, the last time—"

"This isn't last time, Cramp. This is the *new* recipe—given to me by an angel from on high—"

"You mean from an insurance agent named Wanda," snarked Karl.

"Wanda?" asked Cramp. "Was she the one all shiny white with the moccasins?"

"The one and only. And she assures me that this new concoction here is going to put this place on the map." Stan spot checked the tap one last time and reached for a frosty mug. Once in position, he pulled back on the handle and braced himself. It took a moment for the beer to make its way through the empty lines before it gurgled forth from the spigot, gracefully filling the stein under the watchful eyes of the soon-to-be known "Lucky Triumvirate," the blessed three who witnessed the First Pouring.

"Gentlemen, I give you . . . Salvation."

"Salvation?" asked Karl and Cramp simultaneously.

"That's the name of the recipe: Salvation."

"Salvation, huh? Blimey."

"Not a bad name, you crafty S.O.B. Kinda catchy."

"I'm told it is market-tested."

The three men looked on, mystified, as Salvation filled the frosty cup. Salvation, to look at it, is quite a beautiful thing. It has a cloudy golden hue with a hint of red. Salvation has a head, thick and white like fermented custard. Salvation is bubbly-smooth and refreshing and delicious. Drinking Salvation makes you feel happy and content, a bit wobbly in the knees, a smidge mumbly in the tongue, and ready and willing to blow through the entire song catalog cover-to-cover at the *Karaoke Kid*. And it gets you drunk.

"On the house, Cramp," offered Stan as he swaddled the tankard in a cocktail napkin and placed it on the counter as gently as one would lay a newborn babe into . . . just about anything. You have to be gentle with those newborns; can't toss 'em around like a pigskin.

Cramp studied the creamy brew in front of him. He was no art connoisseur. Nor was he a philosopher, or a poet, or a runway-model photographer. He was just a deli man who wouldn't know beauty if it handcuffed him naked to a barnyard animal and painted his balls burgundy. But for one fleeting moment, a singular blip of time, Cramp Holden, the Last of a Long Line of Deli Men, witnessed—somewhere in between those sublime little bubbles marching mesmerizingly up the sides of the glass—pure, unadulterated, unblemished beauty.

Blimey.

Without any further hesitation, Cramp reached out, clasped the glass firmly in his right hand, and steadily raised it to his lips. Eyes closed in meditative reflection, he quaffed Salvation in seven deliberate, dignified gulps. After the last drops of Salvation had been drained, he placed his cup down reverently upon the bar. The corners of his mouth turned upwards as he let out a sigh. It was not the uncouth sigh bellowed by breath-holding competitioners, or the depressing sigh of a disappointed debate-team coach. It was one of those sighs that feels so big and round and wonderful that it can't be dispelled right away and all at once, one that gets stuck right around the voice box and has to be eased out slowly like an art critique. A single tear rolled down Cramp's ruddy cheek.

"So . . . what do you think?" asked Stan coyly, unsure if Cramp had enjoyed his latest attempt at brewery, or if his good friend and deli man was in the opening death throes of some unforeseen poisoning.

Cramp paused and reflected. "Hit me again."

"I'll have whatever this S.O.B. is having."

• • •

"I don't see what was wrong with the old ones."

"Stan, please tell me you are joking. Did you see what you were using to hold your drinks?"

"Of course I did. I was the one who bought them in the first place."

"Buying them and *cleaning* them are two different things."

"I cleaned them . . . sometimes."

"With *water?*"

"Wanda, I don't see what the big deal is. The alcohol kills anything that needs killing anyway. Besides, I think the moss makes them easier to grip. Plus, do things my way—the *Stanford's* way—and you never have to buy new glasses. Given enough time, the glassware will sprout offspring."

"The big deal, Stan, is that this church is now under the direct supervision of the Company—represented by me—and *I* say that we need new glasses."

"But Wanda—"

"Did we not give you the recipe for Salvation?"

"You did."

"And is it not selling faster than you can brew it?"

"It is."

"And is the church not only no longer in any danger of being repossessed by the bank, but also turning a solid profit with every financial forecast predicting a future filled with nothing but profits à la mode?"

"Yes, yes, and yes."

"And are we not spreading the good word about Salvation to more and more people every day?"

"We are."

"And is this not exactly what you wished for?"

"It is."

"And has the Company—have I—ever asked anything of you, made you change the way you do business?"

"You haven't."

"Then what is the problem, Stan?"

"It's just . . . you're right. I'm sorry. I guess some new glasses wouldn't signal the end of the world."

"There we go, Stan. I knew you and I would see eye to eye on this. We think that it's high time *Stanford's* increased its profile."

"And how do new glasses factor into this new profile?"

The new glasses were just the first of several initiatives folded into a carefully crafted marketing campaign spearheaded by Wanda to turn Stan, *Stanford's,* and Salvation into household names like Coca-Cola or Bob Villa. The cornerstone of the operation was getting Stan's mug on every mug, pint glass, T-shirt, billboard, and boob tube as was inhumanly possible.

"The glasses are the key. From now on—and I can't stress how imperative this is, Stan—every drop of Salvation *must* be served in an official *Stanford's* pint glass, frosty mug, or drinking boot. It's important to create . . . brand . . ."

"Dependency?"

"Let's call it . . . loyalty. It's important to create brand loyalty. Plus, it's in your contract. You have no choice in the matter."

Wanda opened a box and began unpacking her marketing campaign.

"Look," she said as she handed him a new official *Stanford's* pint glass. "It's even got your cute, little face on it. Don't worry. I had the guys down in creative airbrush out all the lumps."

"My face isn't lumpy!"

"Not on the pint glass, it isn't."

Stan had to admit, the new official *Stanford's* pint glass was actually pretty snazzy. Somehow they had managed to make his face look . . . appealing, something a lifetime of photographs had balked at attempting to do. Above his smiling profile was written "Salvation" in subconsciously winsome lettering.

"Everything is market-tested up the wazoo. The font, the coloring, the text size, text angle, proportionality in relation to your face, the smell—"

"The lettering has an odor?!"

"Just a hint of pretzel. And your face smells like pepperoni. Give it a whiff." Stan brought the glass to his nose. His nostrils flared as they filled with marketing innovation.

"Great Scott! My face *does* smell like pepperoni!"

"All of it designed to work in concert to subconsciously scream *Drink Me!*"

"Wow, you guys have really put a lot of thought into this, haven't you?"

"When I'm done with you, Stan, your face will be synonymous with—"

"Pint glasses?"

"No."

"Household names?"

"Have you been listening to me at all?"

"What then?"

"Your face will be synonymous with Salvation. And once that happens we will *really* be rolling in it."

• • •

And so Stan got his first taste of the Great Material Hemoglobin. He was by no means vampire-sucking success directly from Dollar Almighty's money veins like the Board of Directors (Salvation enters a solid state at minus-forty degrees, making it a chore to drink and even more difficult to sell) but Stan was more than happy to tipple prosperity from the eye dropper Wanda so adeptly provided with her business acumen.

Stanford's was a success, and Stan himself had attained a certain degree of celebrity—not as much as an action movie star but more than the President of the United States, Moons, and Planets of America—which was plenty for Stan. Every night patrons lined up eagerly at the door, waiting for that five o'clock hour at which they could fill their cups with Salvation and drown their worries in beer. And empty their wallets.

Business was going so well, in fact, that there was even talk of expansion. Stan suggested they install an extra tap to help with the growing demand. Wanda insisted they franchise and set up shop in Milwaukee. Milwaukeeans don't even have a word for "drinking" in their aboriginal tongue. Instead, the verbs *enjoying, walking, sitting around, watching, sleeping, swimming, being, diving,* and *driving* were simply understood to also include the act of drinking alcohol. Those daft cheeseheads can drink transitively *and* intransitively. Wanda guaranteed they would clean up.

And a modicum of success suited Stan. It was good for his overall well-being, not to mention his complexion. Too busy to drink in earnest, gradually and without any real conscious effort, he tapered his drinking down from historical levels to almost-acceptable-in-public levels, leaving his face a shade less sallow. Stan learned something astonishing about drinking: It doesn't always make things better. Alexander may have been Great, but just imagine what kind of title he could have earned had he laid off the sauce for a few minutes: Alexander the Magnificent,

Alexander The Shit, Alexander the Dog's Bollocks. We'll never know. The bum barely made it past Persia.

Stan the Bartender was just fine as far as he was concerned. As fate would have it, he had a knack for the job, as well. He would listen to his flock as they matriculated in, outlining their problems, sharing their good fortune, adding their two cents. And as he listened he would placate their thirst with a smile and hand-crafted, ice-cold wisdom.

"What do you think they should run here, Stan?"

"Hmmm. I think some type of misdirection play—a reverse, maybe. Only by splitting the defense in two will they be able to truly know which player is the real leader on that side of the ball."

"You are wise, Stan."

"There are only five pretzels and two desiccated salt cubes left, Stan. And we are many. How will we feed ourselves?"

"Take those pretzels and desiccated salt cubes and pass them around; and worry not, for the stocks will be forever replenished. It's Karl's job."

"Sage advice, Stan. Spot on."

"Who should I vote for governor, Stan?"

"Go with the dead guy. He's got to be better than any of these other ass clowns."

"Couldn't have said it better myself."

Even Karl began to show signs of cleaning up his carnival act. He finally got off his high-surface-tension ass and starting helping Stan around the bar—as long as *Dallas* wasn't on. Heck, he even let Cramp hold the remote every once in a while—as long as *Dallas* wasn't on.

Lulu was out of debt, off the financial hook, and pulling in some good dough as the principle owner of *Stanford's*. She continued her work at the hospital despite the fact that she didn't need the money; it was what she loved and did best. (All of her patients were head-over-heels to get the fat back on their pork chop.) She did, however, hire a private bus to make the traffic jams on Aldrin just a little bit more palatable. And not having to worry about her brother at all times really cherried her sundae.

Cramp Holden, the Last of a Long Line of Deli Men, found a reason to go on living as the jocular meat slicer he had always been. He was able to put his little mid-life crisis behind him. Stan suspected this might have something to do with the fact that his new business manager had recently begun spending quite a bit of time at the deli next door. Perhaps Wanda, with whom liaisons had dwindled from fewer to none of late, had decided to go straight to the source for her corned beef. And her other needs. But this didn't bother Stan as much as he thought it would. Maybe it was for the best. It certainly cut down on his hospital bills. All in all, life was good.

But life can be a real kick in the armpit like that. Just when you think nothing could muck things up—*kablamo*—you get a visit from some cracked religious zealot.

XV

___

INTUITION

"So what do you need the cricket bats for?"
"Figh'en."
"I see. And the bowler hats?"
"Just in case it rains."
"What about the umbrellas?"
"Figh'en."

• • •

KARL, WHAT are these two beers doing just sitting on the bar?"

"They're for those two fellas in the corner. Ordered those two pints about twenty minutes ago."

"Twenty minutes?! What are you waiting for, Karl? Give those two gentlemen their beers. We here at *Stanford's* may not be known for cleanliness, atmosphere, entertainment—

or for that matter, even service—but I stake our reputation on guaranteeing that our beer will not wallow on the counter for days on end like a lethargic hippo before being served to our loyal customers."

"Oh, believe me, Stan. I tried to give them their Salvations right away, but they weren't having any of it."

"What are you talking about? Who orders Salvation and then just lets it languish on the bar without drinking it?"

"They said they're from Angland, or some such place."

"Angerland? Where in Tarnation is Angerland?"

"I thought it was an island of sorts."

"Angerland is an island?"

"Well, not if it's in Tarnation, it isn't."

"Where the hell is Tarnation, Karl?"

"How should I know, Stan? *You're* the one who started going on about it—wherever it is."

"It's not even a real place!"

"Where? Angland?"

"Tarnation, you twit! *Tarnation* isn't even a real place."

"If Tarnation isn't a real place, then where are those two fellas in the corner from, huh?"

"*You* said they're from Angerland."

"So where in Tarnation is Angerland?"

"Karl, goddammit, why are two pints of Salvation just sitting here on my bar?!"

"I told you, Stan. Those two fellas are from Angland— wherever that is—and apparently in Angland, some people like to drink their Salvation at room temperature."

"They drink their Salvation warm?"

"That's what they told me. I told them that we only sell Salvation ice-cold, but that if they wouldn't mind waiting a bit, I would set aside a couple of pints to warm for them."

"Salvation at room temperature, huh? To each his own, I guess."

"They seem nice enough, although their accents make conversation a bit wonky. They did mention that they were eager to meet you, though."

The two gentlemen from Angerland strolled over to pick up their warm Salvations and introduce themselves to Stan. Word of the Man Who Sells Salvation On Tap had migrated all the way down to the little Earth island of England, which it turned out was spelled with an "E" instead of an "Anger."

• • •

England, Stan learned, was a little country that had to share an island with a few other little countries whose citizens were not often tickled pink to be situated in such proximity to their English neighbors, whom they saw as being "overly overlordly." This led to a whole lot of bickering, quibbling, and mountains being made out of molehills, which history tells us served as the blueprint for the modern democratic process. And a lot of fighting.

Other than hyperbolic deliberation and warm beer, England could be summed up thus: A dapper little nation, whose inhabitants all wear identical bowler hats and carry around umbrellas in one hand and cricket bats in the other, situated on an island a decent swim away from Europe. Although technically "European," the English claim to be part of Europe only when it is fashionable; English people are European in much the same way every American slob with a green sweater and a black eye is Irish. Despite being handicapped with poor food, lousy weather, and chivalry, England did manage, at one time, to attain the rank of Supreme Guv'na of the planet Earth for a good chunk of time, controlling a vast colonial empire. Nowadays all they've got is the Falkland Islands. Although somewhat saddened by their waned world power, they really aren't all that fussed about it, and are generally relieved not to be viewed by their international neighbors as the biggest pricks on the planet anymore—a mantle they expertly passed onto their American brethren—content to let their legacy stand on its own merit. They are the nation which gave us industrial-grade pollution, serial killing, and the YMCA. They have kings and queens and even their own money.

• • •

Stan was beginning to enjoy the company of his new English mates. They were colorful chaps whose outlook on life included the view that anything bad that happened— whether through one's own direct, deliberate actions or completely on a whim—was "unlucky" and therefore no one's fault, certainly not one's own. If you ate a bad piece of sushi—*unlucky*. If you drank your weight in vodka-Red Bulls and consequently got beaten to within an inch of your life for confusing the passenger seat of some random bloke's BMW for the loo—*unlucky*. The clap—*unlucky*. It was all very refreshing and inculpable.

Unfortunately, some of the burly longshoremen who frequented *Stanford's* did not find these Englishmen's ways so appealing. They found them offensive and blasphemous.

"Would you look what we have here, boys," interjected a giant brute with Popeye forearms and a face like a Rottweiler. He was a foreman down at the space port. "Looks like we've got us a couple of gents who seem to be in the wrong establishment. What do you think, Lenny?" He turned to the man next to him, similar in build and demeanor to the foreman, only slightly more burly, unkempt, and scarred.

"I think," began Lenny, "that this isn't the type of place to be sipping your Salvation *at room temperature*." The growing mob grimaced en masse at the mere thought of anyone drinking Salvation warm. Salvation was to be drunk ice-cold or not at all. Although they were hopelessly outnumbered, the Englishmen didn't flinch. They each took a measured swig from their warm pint and turned to face the dock worker mob, ostentatiously adjusting their bowler hats and making conscious note of where their cricket bats lay.

"I don't know about you fellas, but where we come from, the only people who do any *sipping* are pansy, little cry-baby *stevedores* like you."

That one really got their dander up. If there is one thing you don't want to refer to a herd of angry dock-wallopers as—if your goal is not to aggravate them further than you already have—it's *stevedores*. *Stevedore* is one of those words that the English language just flubbed. Just about every word in English, excluding those drab but necessary grammatical place-holders, has a synesthetic quality to it; words feel and sound like they mean. It's really quite extraordinary. This is why, simply by saying it out loud, the word *falderal* brings to mind an annoying academic, the word *grandiloquent* brings to mind the word *falderal*, and the word *guacamole* makes you hungry for something squishy and green. *Stevedore,* on the other hand, brings to mind appletinis and feathered caps, which for some reason doesn't sit well with longshoremen who have spent centuries cultivating a reputation as derelict, unshaven, booze-swilling man's men. So although you may be calling a spade a spade— longshoremen *are* stevedores—you had better put your dukes up.

"This is the last chance for you two to walk out of here wearing your noses," warned the foremen, temporarily keeping his men at bay. "And spread the word: Local 297 says there is only one way to drink Salvation, and anyone who thinks differently is going to have a very painful problem. Lenny, tell 'em how we drink Salvation in 2-9-7."

Lenny took a step forward and stared down the two Englishmen like a gunslinger at high noon. "Ice-cold . . . with exactly one inch of head."

"Lenny, what the hell are you talking about?" snapped the foreman. "You bonehead. It's ice-cold, *just enough head to cover the top*. That's the only way to drink Salvation—that's how Stan pours it."

"I don't know, Fritz," said Lenny in a puppy-dog voice. "When Karl is behind the bar he always pours an inch of head, for aesthetics and what not. It's pretty good. Makes the Salvation a little creamier." Half of the mob began nodding their heads in agreement with Lenny.

"Lenny, you back-stabbing Philistine, that's not how Local 297 drinks Salvation. We drink it the *proper* way—ice-cold, *no* head." The other half of the mob grunted their assent.

"Well maybe there isn't just one way to drink Salvation, Fritz," said Lenny. "Did you ever think of that? You go on and drink it your way and I'll drink it mine—ice-cold *with* head."

The mob divided like a ripened zygote, with those who believed that Salvation could be enjoyed ice-cold with minimal head behind Fritz the Foreman on one side, and those who preferred their Salvation ice-cold with a full inch of head behind Lenny on the other—leaving the Englishmen, who believed in room temperature Salvation, to brawl on two fronts.

"Before this thing gets messy," suggested one of the English blokes, "do you think I might persuade some of you gentlemen to try my beer here. I guarantee, once you've had your Salvation tepid, you'll truly see the light."

"Gimme that," said a man from the Lennian faction. "Let's see what all the hoopla is about." The ruffian swiped a warm glass off the table and swilled the lukewarm suds cautiously. "You know guys, this isn't half bad."

"Hey, let me try!" cried one.

"Save some for me!" bawled another.

"So is that room temperature *with* or *without* head?" posed a third.

A scuffle ensued, evolved into a brouhaha, which in turn segued into a no-holds-barred Donnybrook before the bell rang and the combatants retreated into their corners to regroup before round two started and things escalated into a Tuesday-night-in-Dublin.

Stan came in from the backroom to see what all the commotion was and found his bar transformed into a battlefield with four separate armies clustered into each quadrant. In one corner, Fritz the Foreman gathered his men, each exposed from the waist down but for their boxer shorts. They were performing a ritual sacrifice of all trousers, slacks, and pantaloons—an homage to their patron pourer that they prayed would curry favor and bring rain. In another corner, men were frantically amassing all the desiccated salt cubes they could get their hands on, hoarding them like late-autumn acorns. The other side of the bar housed two platoons of bar regulars whittling pews into cricket bats. Each of Stan's new English mates, who agreed on the proper temperature of Salvation but had had a falling out over the head, was barking woodworking orders to their respective legions. Nobody else knew how the hell to make a cricket bat.

Stan found the whole situation very troubling. Pews don't grow on trees, you know. They are made *from* trees, which take years and years to grow. Growing trees was expensive, and that cost would undoubtedly be passed on to Stan when he was eventually forced to purchase new pews. That was going to cost a lot of money—which didn't grow on trees, either.

"What in Tarnation is going on?!" roared Stan. The bar went as quiet as church wind.

"Stan! Thank the Beer you are here," greeted Fritz. "You can settle this for us, once and for all. Put these blasphemers in their place, will you?"

"Fritz, what in the name of naked legs are you blabbering about? What happened to my bar?"

"Just tell 'em, Stan. Tell 'em that they have to drink their Salvation *ice-cold, without* head."

"Huh?"

"And that as punishment for their transgressions they will all have to be burned at the stake."

"Burned at the stake?!"

"Too much? Well—at least some type of punitive fine, then. Those pews don't grow on trees, you know."

Stan could not believe what he was hearing: burning at the stake, punitive fines. What was next—eternal damnation? Surely it wouldn't come to that.

"Tell 'em, Stan," urged Fritz. "The most important thing about Salvation are the rules and procedures. Everyone knows that there is one—and only one—way to do anything. Life isn't like skinning a cat. Salvation is no different. Rules don't exist to be flippantly disregarded."

"But who gets to make the rules, Fritz?" asked Lenny.

"The rules are made by Stan, of course. It's his bar."

"And when Stan isn't around to mediate, who makes the rules then?"

"Isn't it obvious? Me. I'm the foreman . . . *and* the pitcher on the bar league softball team," replied Fritz matter-of-factly.

"And how do *you* know what Stan would want?"

"That's easy. I can . . . intuit what Stan would want . . . by virtue of the amount of time I have spent cooped up in this bar."

Lenny wasn't having any of it. "I spend just as much time in this place as you do, and I say if there is any intuiting to be done around here, then I'm the one to do it!"

"You're both way off," blurted one of the Englishmen. "*I* am the one who gets to intuit the rules because *I* am the one with the cricket bat."

"You call *that* a cricket bat? Looks more like a club to me—and a poorly whittled club, at that."

"Poorly whittled or not, I'd say it trumps those skivvies you're parading around in. Those piddly little salt cubes, too. What are you gonna do, season me to death?" He had a point there. "Put that in your pipe and intuit it."

"Just hold on there, mate," jumped in the second Englishman. "You're not the only one with a cricket bat—er—club here."

Round two was set to ensue when a fifth belligerent entered through the front door. In most situations like this, with such gripping theater playing out in the middle of the bar, no one would have noticed someone slipping in through the front door. But this new fellow didn't slip. He made quite the entrance—butt naked and yodeling like a black-n'-white Injun brave.

"A-YE-YE-YE-YE-YE-YE-YAH!"

That got everyone's attention.

"Children of sin, moral vagrants, sacrilegious chaff of mankind—here me now, so that I might divert you onto the righteous path to Valhalla!"

But then again, attention can be overrated—and dangerous— if it is just used to piss other people off.

This new character didn't have on a shred of clothing except for an orange Balaclava. Below the neck, he left nothing to the imagination except for the patch of flesh over his heart, which was obscured from view by the bundled stack of orange brochures he cradled in his arm like a marble rye. Everyone imagined that he was hiding a nipple and maybe a few chest hairs behind the orange façade.

"I'm sorry, sir," said Stan. "But I'm going to have to ask you to put away your ding-a-ling."

"Are you bothered by the natural beauty of the nude form?"

"It's not that. It's a health violation. What if it gets into somebody's drink?"

"The laws of Man be damned. I follow a separate code—the one true law."

"Well that's all deep-fried and doughy, but I doubt your one true law is going to re-certify me in the eyes of the county health board—"

"Salvation," he continued, addressing the entire bar, "is like the wind: It blows. Hither and thither, in and out, up, down, and all around. You can try to intuit the rules that govern it until you're blue in the face, but your best bet is to just lick your finger and stick it out the window."

That got their attention again.

"Allow me to paraphrase, if I may, what I'm sure everyone else in this room is already thinking," volunteered Fritz. "What the *fuck* are you trying to say?" He enunciated the "ck" on the fuck in clear staccato fashion. Nudie McCryptic failed to pick up on this phonetic cue. He did not properly gauge the enmity he was cultivating.

"I'm trying to say just this: Let me be your finger. Lick me and I will show you which way the wind blows."

Fritz cold-cocked the newcomer in the area he imagined his nose was hiding underneath the Balaclava, catapulting the bundle of orange brochures skyward and spraying them in every direction, littering the air like Dutch confetti. They had only one thing written on them:

Just have sex as much as and with whomever you like!

Undeterred, the man peeled himself off the floor, refusing to dust himself off.

"You see what all this drinking has done to you. It has made you quick to anger. Just take a step back and look at yourselves, gentlemen: confused and angry, rigging up makeshift weapons out of furniture—"

"You're the one prancing around in your birthday suit!"

"—arguing over the correct way to drink Salvation when the only rule you have to follow is staring you right in the face. Follow me, join the Church of Chad, live as the bonobo ape, and cement your place among the Omniscient Shield Maidens of Valhalla."

By the time he finished his speech everyone had had just about enough of this bozo. The man nearest the Chadic zealot shut him up for good with a cricket club to the knee cap, and nobody said another word about it. Who had ever heard anything so ludicrous?

The bell rang and the brawl to determine who was most qualified to intuit the rules for the correct method of drinking Salvation entered round two. It was doozy of a round.

Stan would have to dole out a lot of money to replace all those pews. He would also, thereafter, make everyone check their cricket bats at the door, make pants a prerequisite for service, and change out all of the desiccated salt cubes for peanuts. Peanuts don't grow on trees, but they *do* grow on the roots of these shrubby, little plants. Close enough.

XVI

REVELATIONS

IV.   *Thou shalt not drive while under too much of The Influence.*

V.   *Just because there is a drain doesn't mean it's Okay to wizz away.*

VI.   *Remember the kickoff time.*

VII.   *Swans a'swimming.*

VIII.   *Look before you swallow.*

IX.   *Mind the gap, not the if-I-do.*

X.   *By virtue of having read all the way down here to number ten, consider your agreement implicitly given and yourself bound to obey all of the above-stated regulations, the breaking of which will subject you to a very hairy hassle. Chug-a-Lug!*

• • •

IN MOST of the grand fables and tales Gumballs Miller had been steeped in as young youth, the protagonist was made to career along a dynamic story arc, taking the hero all the way to Hell and back again. Those types of story arcs really gave the hero moxie. Any character willing to prance into the depths of Hades and hardy enough to make it a return trip, whether motivated by love, loyalty, or a hankering for a piece of triple-fudge chocolate-lava cake, earned his title of *Hero*. Gumballs was no hero. His story did not arc. Nor did it swoop, slope, pivot, bend, yaw, crimp, or curl. Gumballs's narrative made a beeline straight for Hell, and once there it plopped its fat ass down and refused to budge. He had made it to Hell, but the "and back again" portion of the script had been lopped off, presumably by Beelzebub, who didn't have the budget to pull off a pricey Hollywood ending. Best to just fade out and call it a wrap.

Or so it seemed. *This has to be Hell, right?*

Gumballs could not fathom a more tortuous fate than the one he was currently enduring. For the last two-and-a-half weeks he had been forced to sit through his own colleagues' filibuster. The opposition, of which he was apparently a member by virtue of nothing more than the number and position of his assigned seat—a microscopic swath of posterior real estate allotted to him by the Powers That Be upon a mercilessly unergonomic hunk of cushionless bench that was to his buns and lower back what shoes were to feet before the advent of arches and the discovery of Left and Right—wanted desperately to avoid a vote on Proposition 842-∑J, which wished to officially define *chocolate cake* as "cake which is the color of, made of, and designed to taste like chocolate." The current speaker, a veteran in the art of avoiding cloture through endless debate, had chosen the recitation of *The Cup is Half Full: The Unabridged Collection of Every Poem Ever Written by Emily Dickinson—Humous* and *Posthumous* to grind the legislative will of the majority into subatomic smithereens. Ms. Dickinson, it seems, had been a busy little bumblebee following her demise; the volume had yet scarcely been scratched. Still, the majority showed no sign of cracking anytime in the coming decade.

"So, explain to me again why we are filibustering this proposition," asked Gumballs to his Esteemed Colleague and eternal bench neighbor, Archibald.

"Gumby, you silly chap, it's quite simple. We simply don't have the numbers. If a vote were ever allowed to happen we would have to chalk this one up in the 'L' column."

"So what side are we on? The one that thinks chocolate cake isn't chocolate cake or the one that thinks it is?"

"It doesn't matter."

"It doesn't matter?! We've been arguing about this ever since I got here!"

"Not arguing—*filibustering.*"

"What's the difference?"

"If we were *arguing* then someone would eventually have to win. *This* way no one gets their feelings hurt. There are no losers."

"But nothing gets done!"

"Quite right, Gumballs, ole chap. Now you are starting to get it."

"But I thought we were supposed to be *governing* the Universe."

"We *are*."

Surely, Gumballs lamented, *this must be Hell*.

For his "sins" he had been cast down into this legislative chamber for the rest of eternity, forced to go through the theatrics of government equipped with only a seltzer bottle to defend himself against the cream pies whizzing through the air like musket balls. The gargantuan clock on the front wall—the first thing he had noticed upon entering the chamber—tortured him and every other lost soul present by serving both to emphasize how precious few moments had plodded along and to remind anyone who might have momentarily forgotten just how long forever was. His colleagues were the worst brand of riff-raff: politicians—many of whom had stumbled upon the profession by way of practicing law. The "leader" of the majestic body, as Gumballs had come to know the man through his infrequent appearances in the Speaker's chair, was nothing more than a coon-skin cap-wearing, surly sack of dung-smelling vulgarity whose only redeeming quality was that he remembered to button the flap covering his unkempt fundament at least half the time.

Not to mention the heat. Who controlled the thermostat around here?

Surely, this must be Hell.

"So I hear you're going to run for Minority Whip," said Archibald, changing the subject. "Not that it means all that much, but just know that you've got my vote."

"Minority what?!"

"I had no idea you had such ambition. You are one brave soul, I'll give you that."

"What are you talking about, Arch? I never said I wanted to be Minority Whip!"

"Yeah . . . but you also were the only person not to say that he *didn't* want the job."

"So . . ."

"So you're running unopposed! Congratulations, Mr. Whip!"

"Why doesn't anyone else want the job?"

"You mean besides the obvious fact that it would ensconce you nipples-deep in the act of active governance?"

Surely, this must be hell.

Finally one of the majority caved and suggested a suspension of debate and a recess. He had to use the john. Though no one would admit it, the rest of the MPs were beside themselves with relief that someone finally had the balls to give in. Poetry is like Cantarella; best not to overdo it.

The chamber quickly evacuated, and the members made their way to the backroom. Gumballs followed the herd into a great hall filled with gleeful courtiers and foppishly dressed servants disseminating hors d'oeuvres and free magazines to weary lawmakers hobnobbing with their brethren senators. A big band ladled "April in Paris" into the air in fat, legato spoonfuls. Humorous anecdotes and dirty jokes floated around the room like beach-balls. You could even get your shoes shined for a nickel. Can you believe that?—a nickel!

Surely, this *couldn't be Hell, could it?*

Before he could struggle to crack that little counter-intuitive nut any further, Gumballs spotted the one thing, at that particular moment, he wanted more than anything else: a bar. All that filibustering had left him parched.

Gumballs ambled resolutely toward the counter with exigent purposes numbering two: One, find out what the hell was going on, where the hell he was, whether the hell or not this was Hell; and two, get himself a much needed drink. Fortunately for Gumballs, he would be able to kill two birds with one cocktail. Columbonian theory holds that bartenders are a great source of alcoholic drinks, and an even better source of information. Nobody talks more than a drunk and nobody listens to drunks more than a bartender. Everyone knows that was the secret to Columbo's success—that and the fact that if he really got stuck he could just go back and watch the beginning of the episode.

"Excuse me, Miss. You don't happen to have a match, do you? I can never seem to find mine whenever I need them. I know I had one just a moment ago . . ." added Gumballs absentmindedly, doing the Macarena with every empty pocket on his person.

"I hope you don't plan on using it to light that cigar," responded the woman behind the bar, looking up only momentarily from the smorgasbord of martinis, low-ball cocktails, and pilsner beers she was preparing. "You can't smoke in here; this is a bar."

"Oh—of course." Gumballs removed the rolled tobacco from his mouth, thankful that someone had stopped him before he had gotten around to actually smoking it. Cigars may give you a sagacious air, but they aren't worth making your meals taste like bitumen slag for the rest of the week.

"And what's with the creepy trench coat, detective? You on a case or something?" cracked the bartender behind a sardonic smile. "My guess is the butler, in the conservatory, with the three-day-old oysters."

Gumballs could only chuckle as he disrobed and pulled up a stool. He watched the bartender work her magic. A breathtakingly stunning twenty-something with jet black hair and doe eyes, she had to be just about the most efficient barkeep Gumballs had ever seen. She greeted every costumer by name as they filed up to the counter, knew their drink, knew just the right thing to say. She encouraged the disheartened, cajoled the incorrigible, flattered the vain, joked with the comedic—all the time giving a clinic on the art of mixology. Not one single order was ever placed, no money ever exchanged, but every drink arrived prompt and in perfect drinking order. The woman was testament to her profession. It was abundantly clear to Gumballs that this was not her first day on the job.

"Sorry to keep you waiting down here on the end," she said as she sidled over to Gumballs's seat. "It can get a little busy during the rush."

"No problem at all, Miss. I could tell you had your hands full. Is it always so busy?"

"Not always. Must have been one hell of a legislative session. I heard there was poetry."

"*The Cup is Half Full—The Unabridged—*"

"Yeesh. Say no more. No wonder everyone has their Irish drinking shoes on."

"I hope you don't mind me saying so, Miss, but you are doing one heck of a job. I don't know if I've ever seen anyone tend bar quite so . . . elegantly before. Did you know every one of their orders by heart?"

"Well, thank you. It's nothing really. People are creatures of habit. When you've been here for as long as I have . . ."

"So you've been here a long time?"

"Since the beginning, or thereabout."

"And just how long is that?"

"Now Mister, you should know not to ask a lady a question like that. I don't even know your name and you're asking how old I am."

Gumballs blushed, ashamed. "You're right, Miss. I apologize." He stood up off his stool to introduce himself properly. "The name is Gumballs Miller. My friends call me Gumby."

"A pleasure, Gumby," she said as she grasped his outstretched hand and batted her doe eyes. "Lucy. I'm the bartender."

"Does this mean that we are friends, Lucy the Bartender?"

"I hope so. Making friends is an important part of the job. Hard to be a Grumpy Gertrude and a good bartender at the same time."

"I suppose you have a point there."

"So what can I do for you, Gumby?" And just like that, the question had been laid out on a platter like a TV dinner. Since that fateful afternoon on the number 32 bus, Gumballs had been consigned, lined, ignored, interrogated, warned, probed, and bullied; but mostly he had just been confused. Could it be that Lucy the friendly, doe-eyed bartender could remedy everything with one simple answer to an even simpler question?

"Lucy, is this Hell?"

Lucy found the question amusing—so amusing, in fact, that she started hacking away like the Marlboro Man.

"Okay, Heaven then. Is this Heaven?"

"Please," gasped Lucy, trying to poach oxygen out of the miniature breaths she was endeavoring to wedge between the suffocating pyroclastic whoops clogging up her oxygen intake. "Please, stop. I need to catch my breath."

"I don't see what is so goddamned funny. I'm serious here."

"You don't see what is so goddamned funny about Hell?" asked Lucy, unable to help herself.

"No, I don't. I just want some answers. Ever since I bit the big one, I've been boffed about like a philanthropic hooker. First the waiting, then the problem with my insurance, then they send me here, then the Dickinson . . ." Gumballs was starting to hyperventilate.

"All right, all right, just slow down," apologized Lucy. "I knew you were new around here, but I didn't know you were *that* new."

"Please, Lucy, just tell me. I must know. Is this—"

"Whatever gave you the impression that this was Hell?"

"Well . . . they said that I was being sent down. They wouldn't let me use the turnstile. And then when I got here it was so hot and uncomfortable. And then the poetry . . . I just assumed—"

"What do they say about assumption?"

"That it's the mother of all f—"

"Assumption is the poor man's chlamydia. They both start with you being lazy and end with you shamefully holding your Johnson." Gumballs was beginning to get that all-too-familiar flummoxed feeling. His breathing began to caper and cavort as he tried to ascertain what he was missing.

"Does this have anything to do with the condoms again? I thought we already went over that."

"Gumby, you silly goose. I'm going to let you in on a little secret: You're not going to find Hell up here—or Heaven for that matter. Nor will you come across Valhalla, or Elysium, or Sto'Vo'Kor, or Shangri-La, or any of those other mumbo-jumbo locales."

"You mean . . . there is no Heaven?"

"How should I know? I'm just the bartender."

"But then . . . where are we?"

"We are where all souls eventually end up after they've had a roll in the corporeal hay—right here, governing the Universe. It doesn't matter who you are or what you did. Everyone ends up here."

"But what about the Dickinson?"

"Nobody said that politics was for the faint of heart. Sure, you'll have to endure your fair share of filibusters, mud-slinging, and bottom feeding, but politics isn't all bad."

"It isn't?"

"Not *all* of it. There's Question Time. They could sell tickets to that; a right good time, that is." Archibald wouldn't shut up about the upcoming Question Time. Maybe things weren't so bad, after all. Still . . .

"But what's the reason for it all? Why do we end up here?"

"Think of it as . . . civic duty."

"Civic duty?"

"Like I said, governance, although it has its upsides, isn't everyone's idea of a mid-morning quickie."

"I should think not. When is the last time you were stood in front of a poetic firing line and impaled with stanzas unending for weeks?"

"Exactly. So they make it . . . mandatory. Kind of like jury duty."

"So this whole production amounts to jury duty?"

"In so many words, yes. Somebody has got to do it and no one would volunteer if given the choice . . . ergo . . ."

"Jury duty." The words smoldered in Gumballs's mouth.

"Civic . . . responsibility might be a better way of putting it."

"Jury duty is the poor man's civic responsibility."

"Aw, cheer up, Gumby. It's not so bad once you get used to it."

"Not so bad?! You just told me that I have jury . . . responsibility for the rest of eternity, and you want me to cheer up?!"

"I didn't say you had to do it for eternity. Just until you move on."

"And how long does that take?"

"Different strokes for different folks. The Universe expands, contracts, expands, twirls . . . round and round we go, and before you know it you've put in a few dozen cycles—"

"A few dozen?!"

"Yeah, just a few dozen or so cycles and you are free to move on."

"Move on to where?"

"How should I know? I'm just the bartender. You move on to the next step."

"You mean you don't know what comes next?"

"Nope. No one does. What would be the fun in that?"

"Well . . . I guess I just assumed—"

"What did I say about assumption?"

"You know what I mean. I just thought this was the end."

"Gumballs, think about it. All we're doing here is administrating the Universe: yea, nay, stall, nap. In the grand scheme of things the Universe is just a speck, a withered dandelion spore on the wind. It's inconsequential when you get down to it. Of course there are bigger and better and more profound things to dip into."

"The Universe is inconsequential?! Are you kidding me?!"

"In the grand scheme of things, yes, all of this doesn't really matter. We are talking about the mysteries of life and existence, the nature of the soul and the value of the self. We are dealing with the wonder of complexity and the simple Truth—with a capital T. This is a journey, and the only way to know what is beyond that yonder hill is to take it one step at a time. We start back there; then we're here; eventually we move on. Wherever that is or whatever happens—your guess is as good as mine. You can't very well know where you've gotten to before you get there. And anyone who proclaims to know anything more about what goes on after all this comes to an end is nothing more than a carpetbagging charlatan. A word of advice: Instead of listening to other people tell you how things are, you might try just going out and figuring it out for yourself. Forget about all that other hooey."

And just like that, it all got a whole lot lighter for Gumballs. His posture straightened and his shoulders lifted as they were unburdened. Hooey can be downright megalithic to lug around—give you a hernia if you're not careful. Columbo was right; just talk to the bartender.

Xanadu.

"At least that's my take on it. But hey, what do I know? I'm just the bartender."

"But then why the big fuss about the insurance and what not?"

"Oh *that*? That's just about money. Everyone's got to make a living, you know, while we wait to move on. Where do you think all those offertory baskets brimming with cash go? To help feed and clothe the poor? *Pffft*."

Money. All that waiting and worrying and litigating. All of it just for money. Figures.

"Well, Lucy the Bartender, thank you for clearing that up for me," said Gumballs, content in knowing all that he needed to know about everything—at least for the time being. "And if it wouldn't be too much trouble I wouldn't mind a pint of whatever it is you have on tap."

Lucy the Bartender smiled and gave a small curtsey. She returned a minute later with a pint of whatever they have on tap at the recess room for the parliamentary congress of the Universe. Gumballs took a sip. It was a bit stale.

"That'll be $13.75."

"Thirteen seventy-*what*?!"

"Don't look at me, Gumby. I don't make the prices. Where else are you going to get a beer around here?"

"But no one else had to pay. I just watched you dole out a hundred drinks and not a single note changed hands."

"All those people had insurance. It covers the bar tab."

"The insurance is to cover the bar tab?"

"Yeah. What did you think it did?"

"Well I just assu— Never mind. I can't pay $13.75. I don't have any money. I left my wallet with my corporeal body."

Lucy gave Gumballs a pitying glance and exhaled like a mother allowing her child to go to the sleepover despite warnings that nothing of the sort would be allowed in the event the D, which was eventually received on the science test, came to pass.

"I'll tell you what. You are new here, and you seem like a nice guy, so just this once—and I mean once—I'll let it slide."

"Oh, thank you, Lucy."

"Not so fast, moneybags. This isn't a charity. I need something in return. I'll give you the same deal I gave the last fella who came in looking for a handout."

"But I already told you, I don't have any money."

"I know. But you do have something that I want. I'm a bit of a collector, you see. I'll make you a deal: I'll trade you this pint here for your insurance policy. I know you've got it on you."

Gumballs didn't have to think twice.

"Done and done." He dug into his breast pocket and fished out the little figurine of the man nailed to a Roman torture device. "You can have it. A fat lot of good it's done me."

Lucy accepted it graciously and examined it in her hand.

"*This* was your policy? Haven't seen one of these in a long time. You didn't have a prayer."

"Tell me about it."

"What'd they get you on? Condoms?"

"That and . . . the soloing. Who knew it could be so damning?"

"Like I said, you didn't have a prayer. I almost pity you enough to let you have another one, on the house."

"You do?" Gumballs started to smile.

"Almost." He stopped smiling. "Next time it's cold hard cash or nothing at all. You'll not get one drop."

"But where am I supposed to get some money? I can't go through a few dozen expansions and contractions of the Universe sober."

"Do what everyone does when they need money. Get a job."

"A job?"

"You know, gainful employment. I hear there is going to be an opening for Minority Whip."

"Minority what?"

"Either that or start giving blowjobs in the bathroom."

"Minority Whip, it is then."

How bad could it be? And if it kept the pints coming, who was he to complain?

"Just to satisfy my curiosity, Lucy, would you mind telling me what the other guy's policy was—the one he traded for a drink. I've only ever seen the orange brochures."

"I'll do you one better. I'll show you. Would you believe that you are drinking out of it?"

"This pint glass was his insurance policy?"

"Yep. That very glass. Pretty snazzy, huh?"

"I'll say. It's a beautiful glass. Must have been a real bear to carry around in his breast pocket, though."

"Oh, you should have heard him complaining about it. He wouldn't quit his belly-aching: *Who carries anything in their breast pocket? And certainly not a pint glass. Pint glasses are designed to be smuggled out in winter jackets, not breast pockets.* Practically had to glass him over the head with his own insurance policy to shut him up."

Gumballs admired the simple elegance of the pint glass in his hand. It read: *Salvation*. He took another sip.

Salvation, you're goddamned right.

Just then his Esteemed Colleague and (not quite) eternal bench partner, Archibald, tapped Gumballs on the shoulder.

"Gumby, ole chap, where have you been? I've been looking everywhere for you."

"I've just been having a drink and a chat with Lucy here. Have you two met?"

"Brandy Old-Fashioned Sour, Archie?"

"Lucy, dear, I would like nothing more than to sample your wares, but there are some people I want Gumby to meet before the recess ends, some of the real movers and shakers in the party, people who can really help with his campaign."

"Minority Whip?"

"Quite right. So then he's already told you?"

"He mentioned it." She gave Gumballs a smile. *That was quick.*

"Now, come on, buddy boy, recess won't last forever. There is not a moment to lose. We've got to procure some yard signs."

"But I haven't finished my drink yet."

"This isn't California! Stop drinking like a cheerleader and get her down!"

Gumballs couldn't argue with that logic. He pressed the glass to his lips and began quaffing his drink like a man. As the beer level measured against the bottom of the pint receded with each gulp, he could slowly make out something written at the bottom of the glass, previously hidden by beer and visible only to the one who had drained it. The print was fine, but luckily Gumballs had died with his bifocals on. Unfashionable as they were, they hadn't failed him in forty-seven years and they wouldn't start now. With his head tilted back at the perfect angle to get at the last dregs of slightly flat beer, Gumballs could make out everything perfectly:

I.   *Salvation® is my brand. It is a registered trademark of Afterlife, Inc. Its recipe is patented. Thou shalt drink no other beer than it.*

II.   *Thou shalt not drink Salvation® in any other receptacle than officially certified Salvation® brand cups, mugs, glasses, pitchers, or boots.*

III.   *Any questions so far? One and Two are the big ones, really*

XVII

FRUITCAKE

It's the end of the world as we know it,
It's the end of the world as we know it,
It's the end of the world as we know it,
And I feel . . .

• • •

STAN WAS too busy to notice that the sun had been blotted out of the sky. Sweat glistened off his brow as he labored behind the bar. At the moment, he was attempting to construct a second beer tap out of an old refrigerator and a bean bag chair he had scavenged from the lot next door. The task required a passing knowledge of welding, metallurgy, and sobriety. Stan had managed to avoid having a drink all morning, but it was becoming crystal clear that his history background was a poor substitute for a welding torch. As the five o'clock hour approached, he resigned himself to having to pay someone who was, at the very least, nominally qualified to take a crack it. He was envisioning some sort of beer barter when his train of thought was interrupted by Lulu bursting in through the front door. She looked like she had just come out of a meeting with her cellular phone provider that had not ended amicably. Her normal glow had dimmed to a clammy, pale complexion, and her hair was phoofed incongruently to one side like Einsteinian bedhead.

"Sister! What a pleasant surprise," he greeted her. "I thought you worked today."

"What are you *doing*!?" she gasped, out of breath.

"I'm trying to build an extra tap to accommodate all the new business. With an extra—"

"I'm not talking about—Are your sure that's what you're doing?"

"It's the first attempt. I admit there are some flaws in the design. Consider it a work in progress." Lulu pitied the lump of mangled refrigerator on the counter briefly before she remembered her original purpose.

"No, no. What are you *still* doing here? Shouldn't you be preparing?"

"I *am* preparing. We open in fifteen minutes."

"You mean you don't know?"

"Know what?" Lulu grabbed the remote control off the bar and clicked on the TV. She didn't even have to change the channel. They were all broadcasting the same thing.

Filling the entirety of the grainy screen was the foreboding outline of a massive attack vessel. It was, according to the newscaster's voice augmenting the picture, roughly the size of the Moon itself, and it had arrived twenty-five minutes earlier from a galaxy unknown, without warning. The only discernible markings were the letters which displayed the name of the apocalyptic spacecraft in fiendish, crimson runes along the starboard side. They read: *HMS Old Testament* (His Merciless Ship—not the Queen's). Both Earth and Moon governments had already fired their entire arsenal of thermonuclear anti-matter bazooka bombs— ordnances which, when tested on a remote asteroid in the bikini belt, the newsman assured, had blown the astrolith straight into last Tuesday—to no effect. The vessel remained unscathed.

Deafening intercom feedback boomed through the atmosphere as the captain of the space cruiser addressed the bastion of Earthling civilization as an elementary-school principal would an auditorium full of snot-hemorrhaging little scholars.

"PEOPLE OF EARTH—AND THE MOON. . . MERRY CHRISTMAS!" There was a pause. "AND MERRY JUDEGEMENT DAY. HO-HO-HO!"

At that moment, there were a great many humans on Earth—and the Moon—who had a thought which could be parathunk like this: *Well, if we are all going to die, at least we finally know that we are not alone in the Universe. Maybe these aliens would change their minds if we played volleyball with them. Does anyone know how to get the whiskey out of this thing?* These romantic dreamers were devastated when the message was rebroadcast, this time with a picture of the man who was giving it. This courier of impending doom was Caleb Wright the Eleventh. He wasn't an alien at all. He was the great-great-great-great-great-great-great-great grandson of Caleb Wright the First, the original founder of the The Faithful 16.

• • •

The Faithful 16 had not had a fairytale existence. After a few generations of meandering aimlessly through uncharted emptiness on the space barge *Mayflower*—which really wasn't much bigger than your average Japanese living room—and guided only by the grace of God—which the convoy soon discovered was as substandard at finding north in space as their Boy Scout orienteering compasses—the intrepid wanderers were eventually fortunate enough to stumble upon a harsh-but-habitable uninhabited moon. New Plymouth colony was founded, a church was built, and everything was A-OK. The first winter was a bit touch-and-go for a while, but by that time the Plymouthians had become experts in hamster husbandry. They were able to sustain themselves on hamster jerky and Puritan elbow grease. They used the hamster pelts to make moccasins and fezzes—very warm in the winter. As the population grew gradually over time, new colonies were settled on neighboring space rocks. New Providence, New New Haven, and Re-York soon joined mother Plymouth as the centerpieces to a burgeoning galactic empire—one in which there weren't any liberals sashaying about like pantywaist thespians. Life was good. And straight.

Now they had returned to the native bosom of the their motherland, but their original mandate of finding and founding a place to practice the pure form of their religion in peace had altered, just slightly. They were now the scourge of the Universe. I tell you, they were worse than kidney stones. They had been infected by a terrible plague which had rendered the entire society a paranoid, militarized zombie mob.

It was Christmas. Christmas had caused the entire colony to go balls-out bonkers. It began harmless enough, with a handful of days off of work and the exchange of a few gifts, but prolonged exposure to the diabolical pestilence acted like a sinister brand of holiday encephalopathy. It ended in genocide.

No one can pin-point exactly where things went all pear-shaped, but most finger the removal of Thanksgiving and New Year's Day from the Plymouthian calender as the beginning of the end. For years, these two holidays had served as stopgaps to Christmas ambition. They had effectively corralled the Christmas season into an exhausting, but manageable, one-month barrage. Without the two bookends, Christmas spread like garden gnomes.

One month of frenzied materialistic mayhem can cause anyone to go a little hinky, but that alone is not enough to send an entire population to the nut house. The music was the real culprit. With every department store, bodega, and radio station pumping maddening Christmas melodies directly into everyone's brain, something had to give. Once it went a capella, nothing could stop it.

By the time Christmas had invaded September, it was already too late. Within a generation, Mega-Clause was worshiped every day of the year. Society crumbled like bad meatloaf. Nobody was allowed to work; everyone was required to buy presents. It wasn't long before caroling raiding parties scoured the dystopian countryside like deranged Scythians, trawling for yuletide booty.

Having laid waste to their entire moon, Plymouthians took to the stars to feed their ever-growing blood lust for ribbons and wrapping paper. The neighboring colonies quickly fell helplessly under the callous jackboot of St. Nick, forced into elven slave-labor camps to build tops and Barbie dolls, or to mine Tickle-Me Elmos, for their covetous overlords. Plymouth had a military advantage over their peace-enfeebled neighbors: fruitcake.

Fruitcakes had been stockpiled since the very first Christmases on the colony. Originally they were treated like spent nuclear fuel rods; society had no use for them but couldn't very well just toss them into the Dumpster for fear they would contaminate the drinking water and cause birth defects. With a half-life of 700 million years and enough booze and candied fruit to render it indestructible, fruitcake was the gift that kept on giving—forever. Each year people bequeathed the insidious bread onto the less-than-likeable members of their extended family only to receive twice the amount in return. The only way to get rid of fruitcake is to eat it; that was out of the question. Sometime shortly after everyone started to go bat-shit crazy, some demented soul figured out a way to weaponize it.

It wasn't long before the entire Plymouthian battle fleet was outfitted with 92-inch cannons—capable of destroying entire communities with greater efficiency than a Walmart yield bomb—and retrofit with fruitcake armor plating. Once the final nonperishable brick had been expertly mortared to the hull by a master mason, the battleship was impervious to any weapon of the day. It wouldn't have mattered if Earth—or the Moon—had launched a bazillion thermonuclear anti-matter bazooka bombs. The shielding on the *Old Testament* was Tupperware tight.

• • •

"Stan, what are we going to do?" Lulu was despondent.

"I don't know. Just give me a second to think about this."

"Shouldn't we get under the table or something?"

"That only works with earthquakes and nuclear bombs. No, what we are dealing with here is a whole 'nother ball of hash. You heard the broadcast. The thermonuclear anti-matter bazooka bombs were as effective as marriage counseling." Stan searched around the bar for his thinking cap. He thought he had left it by the bean bag chair. "Lulu, have you seen my thinking cap around here?"

"The fez?"

"Yeah, you know, the furry one."

"Fuck your furry fez, Stan! We've got to get out of here!" She was starting to lose it. Ear-splitting explosions could now be heard with increasing regularity as the city around them was peppered with 8,000-caliber warheads. Stan could feel his own resolve fraying. He needed to do something responsible, and quick.

"First thing's first; we need a drink." Before Lulu could raise any protest, two frosty mugs of ice-cold Salvation lay bubbling away on the bar counter. Lulu disregarded her usual aversion to alcohol and quaffed the tankard with frat-boy zeal. Stan had barely begun work on his before she slammed the empty mug down.

"Thanks. I needed tha—Wow, that's fantastic, Stan! I despise beer but that was liquid manna. Did you make that?"

"I *told* you. This new recipe is the real deal. Hit you again?"

"What the hell. It's the end of the world as we know it. Why not? Lay another—What do you call this stuff?"

"Salvation."

"Lay another Salvation on me, my fine bartending brother."

As she sipped her refill at a more leisurely pace, Lulu could not get over how calm she felt. The world, the Moon, her life—were all coming crashing down like a kamikaze coffee buzz, but she couldn't remember a time when she had felt more at peace. Her feet skipped over to the juke-box. She found herself in the mood for some 1980s alterna-tive rock—Athens, Georgia-style. Just as she was about to make her selection, the front door detonated off its hinges.

Karl stood in the doorway. His clothes were in tatters; everything from the waist up—which accounted for 97 percent of his total body mass—was shredded. A gash above his right eye was trickling crimson onto his dusted face. He looked like a tomato that had been hastily mummi-fied in the midst of a dry-walling typhoon. A frenzied mob of people in a similar condition huddled behind him.

"Stan! Are you a sight for sore eyes! Thank G—This place is still standing? It's a miracle. The rest of the block is rubble. You—Are you drinking?"

"Yes, I am, Karl." Stan was using his guru voice.

"Me, too," piped in Lulu, holding her suds high for all to see. "Cheers, Karl—ya big lug."

"Of all the times you could have chosen to get drunk you choose—Is that—"

"—Salvation. Yes, it is, Karl. Would you care for one?"

"Would I." He limped over to his usual perch.

"One Salvation, coming right up. Everyone, please come in! The doors to *Stanford's* are open to all. Come in out of the carnage and take your mind off the worries of the world." He motioned for the mob to enter. They were a sorry looking lot, if ever he had seen one: dirt and grime from head to toe with the odd appendage missing here and there.

"First round of Salvation is on the house!" The cheers went up like static-charged hydrogen.

"Bless you, Stan!"

"You're a saint!"

"Three cheers for Stanford Adam!"

The jukebox revved up and drowned out the apocalypse all around them. Earth—and the Moon—were being fruitcaked into coffee grounds, but inside *Stanford's* Salvation brimmed in every patron's cup. People had never been happier. It was the end of the world as they knew it . . . and they felt just peachy.

> *The other night I dreamt of knives, continental drift divide.*
> *Mountains sit in a line*
> *Leonard Bernstein.*
> *Leonid Breshnev, Lester Bangs, and Lenny Bruce.*
> *Birthday party, cheesecake, jelly bean . . .*

EPILOGUE

BOOM!

ON EXCLUSIVITY
A note from the Author

If you are reading this, it means you've finished reading my book; and in my book, at least, that makes you all right. Reading books requires a great deal of time—time which you could have just as easily spent reading other books or sea kayaking or taking internet yodeling lessons—and I am beside myself with gratitude that you decided not to ditch this thing mid-read and instead stuck it out. I'm going to go out on a limb just a little bit and take the fact that you are *still* reading it— because, let's face it, how many people actually read these little addendums?—as a sign that you liked the book enough not to hate it. Hopefully you are thinking to yourself something along the lines of: *You know, this wasn't half bad. I enjoyed this at least as much as, say . . . watching re-runs of* Matlock *or dieting. I wonder what this fellow is going to say here at the end?* Perhaps you even enjoyed it. I do hope so.

I have the pleasure of informing you that in slogging your way all the way here to the back, you have initiated yourself into the ranks of an exclusive literary circle: You are now one of a select few individuals who have not only heard of *The Gates of Valhalla,* but have actually read the blasted thing. I commend you.

Exclusivity is generally a good thing. It's glorious when it applies to club memberships or scandalous celebrity interviews or banking passwords. Unfortunately, it is decidedly less remarkable when it is the defining characteristic of your literary footprint—if your goal is to sell books, that is. People hardly ever buy books whose existences is unknown to them. You can take that to the bank.

And while you are there, you may notice the conspicuous absence of one thing in particular: namely, people who are me cashing fat royalty checks.

The reason for this is because *The Gates of Valhalla* is my debut novel. I am known to the general public about as well as the second line to *Moby-Dick.* I am the poor man's Michael Collins (google "Apollo

11"). This has, in turn, made my readership "exclusive," which is really just a euphemism for "Jasper *Who*?!"

But everyone has to start somewhere; I am hoping to start with you, O valued reader.

So if you have enjoyed reading this humble volume, if it has tickled all the right bones and left a warm, chuckley sensation in your guts, if you have deemed its reading a worthwhile use of your invaluable time, I would really be quite chuffed if you might tell someone about it.

I could really use your help in this regard. You, you see, are the sum total of my entire marketing campaign. Other than the website and the odd 140-character sprinkling of self-important puffery, you're pretty much all I've got. So any assistance at all that you might be willing to lend in the general area of getting the word out about this book would be greatly appreciated.

I'm not looking for a ten-page review by any means—though those are welcome—just a few seconds of extra effort. Something as simple as just rating this book on your e-reader (or wherever people put stars next to book titles, really) would be of immense help. If you are willing to go the extra yard and post a sentence or two—perhaps something to the effect of: *On a scale from 1 to Good, I sh*t my pants* or *Even better than* Matlock*!*—you'll have me doing cartwheels.

I'll take any publicity I can get, actually. Feel free to mention the book anywhere that involves: handles, hashtags, followers, water coolers, break rooms, cafeterias, bulletin boards, soapboxes, fliers, megaphones, or nationally syndicated mass media programs. If you would like to decorate your left buttock with a *Gates of Valhalla* commemorative tattoo, I will not stop you—although, I might encourage you to consider a rewarding career in the adult-movie industry.

Understand that my desire for less exclusivity is not an altruistic one: I doubt very much that you will get anything more out of this book than you haven't already now that you've gone and read it. Have no illusions about it; I am advocating this comprehensive campaign of shameless self-promotion purely for my own personal (monetary) gains.

In short, I want money and fame and notoriety. That is all, really. I think it would be a sweet deal if I could just write books like this one for something close to a living. Fat chance—I know—but you can't blame a guy for giving it the ole college try.

So what do you say? How's about giving your ole pal Jasper a hand?

Of course, if you really can't be bothered to do anything I won't hold it against you. I can't say that I myself spend that much time making other people money when there is nothing in it for me—I'm American, for chrissake. I will just use the knowledge that someone has read (and enjoyed?) something I have written to warm my soul when I'm chattering my teeth off in the bread line next Valentine's Day. I'll take a warm soul over a winter jacket any day.

Thank You Kindly,

—Jasper Grawl

www.jaspergrawl.com
@JasperGrawl
(#GatesofValhalla)
Fans of Jasper Grawl on Facebook

About the Author

Jasper Grawl is an English teacher and copy writer living in Tokyo, Japan. He is a Badger, a graduate of the University of Wisconsin—Madison with a degree in The Art of Making Mountains out of Molehills. His diploma calls this field "Political Science."

The Gates of Valhalla is his debut novel.

www.JasperGrawl.com
Facebook: Fans of Jasper Grawl
Twitter: @JasperGrawl
Goodreads: Jasper Grawl
e-mail: FansOfJasperGrawl@gmail.com.

The Fresh Ink Group

Publishing
Free Memberships
Free Stories, Essays, Articles
Free-Story Newsletter
Writing Contests

Books
E-books
Amazon Bookstore

Authors
Editors
Artists
Professionals
Publishing Services
Publisher Resources

Readers' Forum
Blogs
Social Media

www.FreshInkGroup.com

Email: info@FreshInkGroup.com

**The Fresh Ink Group is a proud member of
The Coalition of Independent Authors and Publishers**

FANTASY PATCH

By Stephen Geez

Picture This!

Danté Roenik creates ad campaigns, reveling in the fine art of rendering his concepts on million-dollar canvasses financed by big-budget clients. Intoxicated by the sheer power of directing public opinion, he dares wage war against the conglomerate behind a worldwide anti-depressant increasingly associated with sporadic violence. To juxtapose his images with reality, he enlists a mixed palette of business tycoons, his fiancée/attorney, a team of corporate-spy soldiers of fortune, one resurgent news anchor, and the best TV-production crew in Chicago.

But the sharp lines dividing perception from truth begin to blur when the darker motives shaping mass media come to light. Forced to re-examine the ethics of designer pharmacology, Danté is painted into a corner, his future about to be erased as patients die, clients lie, and unhealthy doses of murder prove too hard to swallow.

Too late to whitewash the stain of deceit, Danté must decide who deserves to appear in his picture, the true subject an unfinished self-portrait way past its own deadline.

It's not what you see, not what you get . . .

But all you could ever imagine.

Let Danté show you how . . .

With a Fantasy Patch!

www.FreshInkGroup.com
ISBN: 978-1-936442-06-5

www.ingramcontent.com/pod-product-compliance
Lightning Source LLC
Chambersburg PA
CBHW020102180626
46812CB00006B/2433